THE CAPTAIN

BY SEYMOUR SHUBIN

ANYONE'S MY NAME

THE CAPTAIN

A NOVEL

SEYMOUR SHUBIN

STEIN AND DAY / *Publishers* / New York

First published in 1982

Designed by Judith E. Dalzell
Printed in the United States of America
STEIN AND DAY/*Publishers*
Scarborough House
Briarcliff Manor, N.Y. 10510

Library of Congress Cataloging in Publication Data

Shubin, Seymour.
The captain.

I. Title.
PS3569.H754C3 1982 813'.54 82-40011
ISBN 0-8128-2880-1

To Neil and Jennifer

Acknowledgment

I want to pay tribute to the late Shirley Fisher who believed in this novel from the beginning and encouraged me to complete it.

THE CAPTAIN

1

Even the police, when they were to come there for the first time, were surprised it was an attractive place. From what some of them had seen at other nursing homes and from the scandals that occasionally broke in the newspapers, they expected something closer to a urinal than a hospital. But it looked like a hospital, and even more: the lobby was plushly carpeted, with handsome furnishings and hangings; and the dining room had something of the hotel look, too, though it was uncarpeted, of course, because the patients—or residents, as the management preferred—often spilled their food.

It was a vaguely Colonial-looking one story brick building, with a long, pillared veranda, and four wings that couldn't be seen from the front. Back there, off the lobby, past the swinging doors, it looked exactly like a bright modern hospital, each of the wings with its own curved nursing station. And back there you would occasionally get a whiff of urine because it was hard to keep up with these people, no matter how much you scrubbed or the air-purifying system toiled. So the police, like most people who weren't exposed to this every day, would suddenly find themselves up against a wall of urine-smell they had to walk through. After the first pleasant feeling about the place, the reality of just what it was came through in the form of lolling figures in their wheelchairs, the gaunt faces, the repeated gestures, the stares. And, like just about every other visitor, most would think or mumble to each other something like, "Kill me if I ever get like that, don't put me away."

The night shift, eleven-to-seven, was generally the easiest for the staff. You would hear an occasional cry or someone would die; of course you had your wanderers, though if someone wandered once you would usually put up the bedrails. But it was generally fairly quiet, like this night on Wing B, so when the nurse came out of the bathroom and back to the station she was startled to see a hulking fully dressed figure down the hall. She quickly put on the glasses she'd been cleaning, and the figure formed into the captain, bald with his round puttylike face and glob of a nose and horn-rimmed glasses. She groaned softly. Jayzus, he hadn't flipped out, too. But she'd seen it happen just like that.

In a way it was worse than being fully dressed, because that had some kind of logic to it; but he had a topcoat over his pajamas, and his ankles were bare and very white above his black oxfords. He stared at her as she approached him. Though he was massive, there was a touch of frailty about him. After all, he was in his seventies.

"And where are you going, Captain?" she asked lightly.

It was several moments before any words came out. "Nowhere. I can't sleep."

"Does anything hurt you?"

"No."

"Are you chilly?"

It wasn't any surprise to her when he nodded. Most of them were cold, even now in July. "Well, why don't you wear your nice robe and slippers?" But she didn't wait for an answer; she had things to do and he appeared pretty clear, not just absently wandering. "I've got an idea. Why don't you just go back to bed and think pleasant thoughts?"

She stood watching as he shuffled off, then went back to her station.

Once he was in his room the shuffle became long strides as he went to the window and peered through the blinds. But he couldn't see to the parking lot. If that fucken jig albino didn't show up or didn't wait he'd put his fist down his throat. He broke away from the window, heart rocketing, and stepped close to the door. But he was afraid to glance out. He looked back at his bed, with the mound under the covers; the most he'd ever seen them do at night was look in from the doorway. In the next bed Elephant Ears looked like a skull that would take off in a breeze; he slept with his tongue hanging out. Now the captain steadied himself against the doorway, about to risk another peek.

You had to be so goddamn patient. That was the trick. Make your move too fast, forget it. A half a million dollars worth of horse, street value, would have been down the toilet that time, and they'd have broken down the door into a roomful of smiles; but he'd said to the boys clustered around the street corner, "Hold it, just hold it, I don't like that car." It was maybe an hour before the car finally moved and he'd motioned them on after him. And later when they'd made the collars and found the horse and picked up the car, they saw it had a telephone.

It was that case, wasn't it?

He thought hard, as though trying to think his way through a brick. Yeah. Sure.

For a few seconds that had caught him up so thoroughly he'd even stopped thinking about the nurse. But the anxiety was back and he eased his head out ever so slightly. He snapped back. All he had to do was get across the hall to the alcove where the soda machines were, but she was sitting there at the station in profile, a pencil to her chin.

Every so often he glanced out. Now, about five minutes later, she was walking away from him down the hall. He drew in a quick breath and stepped out and strode over to the alcove without looking to either side. He stood there, his breath coming in painful gasps. Slowly he opened the door to the storeroom, then reached into his pocket for the key to the outside door. If that fucken albino got him a bum copy. . . . But the lock turned.

Outside, with the door closed behind him, he felt as though caught in a prison yard spotlight. But it was just the lights around the place. It was a hot night, but he felt cold as he hugged the wall around to the parking lot.

Which car? Which, if any?

He stepped into the middle of the lot, and as he did headlights flashed on. The car came toward him, the door swung open and he got in. It wasn't until they got out to the street that the driver spoke.

"You're gettin' me in trouble, Captain."

He didn't say anything. Instead he took a slip of paper from his pocket and handed it over. He couldn't always trust his memory, so he'd written down the address. In fact, he'd written it down three times because he wanted to make sure it was clear. The albino studied it against the dashboard lights. The captain looked at his puffy face: it was a sickly yellow-cream color, with a touch of freckles; there was also a hint of red in the white wool of his hair. Some of the best boys on his squad were jigs, he thought. But they weren't this crazy color, and they didn't take it up the ass.

Not that fruits bothered him. As long as they didn't go after kids or him or anyone who didn't want it. And if you let them have their little wrong they made good stoolies. But that was the secret with all stoolies. You can have your little wrong as long as it ain't violent or dope or any real felony, and you kept your wires open. Christ, who'd had more wires than him?

"Captain, I ain't sure where this is. I got an idea, but I ain't sure. You know where it is?"

If he got close he'd know. Fast: "C'mon, c'mon, get the hell outta here!"

"What you want to go there for this late?" he said, driving. When he didn't get an answer, "You gonna be there long, Captain?"

"No."

They drove in silence. After a while the albino said, "Captain, you really got me wrong."

"Bullshit."

"I'd have driven you anyway. You didn't have to say what you did. I never touched one of them old folks. Ain't I good to them? Don't I clean up their shit? Why were you gonna say I did?"

"Don't you ever touch 'em, you hear? You and that bimbo in the kitchen can fuck yourselves dry but don't you touch no one else."

"Christ, Captain."

He'd sensed the weak one right away. The bimbo cook looked like he wouldn't bend, but the albino had that certain weakness about him. And after waiting for him to finish taking some of the people to the shower, he took him aside and told him. He didn't tell him he'd seen him with his hand on the bimbo's ass. Just that he was going to the office because he'd caught him with No Voice, that poor bastard.

"I think we're here, Captain."

For the past few moments the captain had been sitting there in a panic. Nothing looked familiar. In fact, he forgot which daughter's house he was going to. Or maybe it was Mark's. No, not Mark. He'd been with Ellen or Rosemarie the last time. God, which had it been, Ellen or Rosemarie?

"Okay, we're there now," the albino said.

And it was coming back to the captain also. Rosemarie.

"Park here."

He got out, trying to orient himself. For a couple of moments he felt some vertigo and grabbed hold of the car. But he was all right now. Only the night light was on in the house, the one they kept on in the living room. He made his way cautiously down the alley to the rear yard, stopping every few moments to try to adjust to the darkness. He touched a fence and knew that the doghouse was to the left. He followed the fence and then saw the outline of the doghouse.

What if it was gone?

He was on his knees, reaching into the doghouse. He had to reach in far. Then his fingers touched heavy plastic. He drew it out and unfolded it. He took out the revolver and the small box of cartridges. He held the revolver in his hand. He pointed it at the house, rage pulsing in his temples. Then he lowered it and wrapped it up again and put it in his pocket for the ride back.

2

Dr. Bennett pulled his two-door Mercedes into one of the four parking spaces reserved for physicians; it was the only physician's car there. He eased himself out, gave a lengthy stretch, then reached in for his sport jacket and bag. He put on the jacket as he walked toward the steps of the home.

"Hello, Dr. Bennett."

"How's it going?" But didn't wait for the young woman at the front desk to reply. Instead he peered around her at the darkened offices just to make sure no one was there. No one was: it was going on six and administration generally left at five-thirty. Just as well. He'd stopped in on his way home and he couldn't wait to be there, to get out of these clothes and into a shower.

He walked back to Wing B, greeted Mrs. Latimore, the RN at the station, and asked for the Finklestein and Manning charts. As he studied them, a couple of the kitchen help were guiding a tray-filled cart through the hall for residents who couldn't eat in the dining room. Someone tugged at his sleeve, a bony plaster-white toothless woman loosely restrained in a wheelchair. "I'm a good girl, Uncle Josh. I'm a good girl."

"I know you are, honey."

He turned back to the charts as an aide guided the wheelchair along the hall. From somewhere came a wail.

He'd gotten a call that afternoon that they believed Mrs. Finklestein had come up with a hernia and that Mr. Manning had some gross hematuria. He had twenty-eight—or was it twenty-nine now?—patients assigned to him, whom he would see routinely once or twice a month. Whenever possible he would give the nurses standing orders. But he was always on call, of course, though generally he could either handle it on the phone or, if it seemed to be an emergency or beyond nursing home care, would have them send the patient to one of the nearby hospitals.

"Mrs. Finklestein, you look so pretty today."

She stared at him from the chair near her window. Mrs. Latimore had followed him in.

"Does anything hurt you?"

"They give me *dreck* to eat."

"I'm not going to hurt you, I just want to examine you."

It was easy to see the swelling in the labium as he examined her in a standing position. He was able to reduce it gently with his fingers and to see that it was above the inguinal ligament, that it wasn't femoral. She couldn't answer if it hurt, but apparently it didn't for she showed no signs of tenderness. Back at the station he wrote "indirect inguinal hernia" on her chart, and the decision would be whether an operation or a truss. In an old person you often had to do a herniorrhaphy, had to strengthen the posterior wall of the canal, in addition to the herniotomy. He couldn't see putting someone in her late seventies through that, though obviously there was always the danger of strangulation. He would try a truss first, although now that he saw it on her chart he recalled that she had extremely sensitive skin. . . . Well, a truss first.

Mr. Manning, though, would have to go to the hospital. From the call, he'd felt they had botched the catheterization again. But among other things he didn't like the feel of the prostate.

Handing back the chart he was tempted to call it quits, but his conscience bit at him and he asked for the nurses' progress notes on all of his patients in the wing. He hadn't been in for nearly a week and he wasn't about to go through all of them, since he would have been called if there was anything serious, so he leafed through the pages for the past couple days and nights. Galtman . . . appetite better; Shoner . . . back in restraints because, oh Christ, peed on his dinner; Jones . . . swelling of ankles went down; the captain . . . 12:16 A.M. yesterday, in hall in coat, pajamas, shoes, but went right back to bed on request, was sleeping when looked in.

Again he was about to leave, but that was so unusual for the captain that he said to Mrs. Latimore, "How's the captain been today?"

She squinted and curled her lips as though in a rage. "Like this. Oh, I'm exaggerating."

"Is he acting up in any way?"

"Hasn't complained today if that's what you mean."

"Let's see his chart." He knew what the captain was taking but wanted to be sure. Could be he was reacting to medication.

"Hughes, Walter, seventy-six," he said in a kind of singsong way as he flipped from the front pages to the back, then looked at the front again. Hydrochlorothiazide, 50 mg in the morning, for hypertension. He'd been taken off Thorazine for severe anxiety but was still on Elavil, 10 mg t.i.d. and 20 mg at bedtime, for depression. Four weeks ago Lomotil for diarrhea, two and a half weeks ago tetracycline for five days for a bug of some kind, *dum, dum, dee dum. . . .* Well, it was hydrochlorothiazide and Elavil now, and though any drug could give a reaction he doubted if there was any connection after all this time. See how it went the next few nights.

Actually, the captain was much improved since he first came here three months ago following gallbladder surgery. The children said they couldn't handle him anymore because he was depressed, would get confused, but who the hell wouldn't if you were bounced from one kid's home to another every three or four months? This wasn't to say there mightn't be some cerebral arteriosclerosis, but he couldn't see any clear features of it. In fact, the medication had eased his depression within a few weeks, and with it his confusion seemed to have lifted. It made him wonder about a lot of doctors; with all that was in the literature they still didn't seem to catch on that it could take weeks for antidepressants to work, that you had to give them time.

But, as often happened to these people when their depression thinned out and they really became aware for the first time of their environment, they became quick-tempered, hostile. Not that the captain was violent; nothing like that. But as one of his daughters said, she had never heard him say anything worse than hell or damn in her life—happened after he got here.

He glanced into the captain's room on his way out. He was lying in bed fully clothed, his big hands locked beneath his head.

"Captain, just wanted to say hello. How you doing?"

The captain stared over at him, chin near his shoulder.

"Not talking today? Take it easy, Captain," and now he was gone.

"Time for dinner, Captain," the albino said.

"I'm staying here."

"You ain't feelin' well?"

"I'm okay."

"They ain't gonna like that."

Another orderly came in shortly. "Mack says you're not going to the dining room."

"So?"

Mrs. Latimore and a nurse's aide followed soon after, but he wasn't leaving. They finally ordered him a tray.

He just drank some tea, lying in bed. He'd had breakfast and lunch in the dining room and they'd made him go to that fucken room where you drew pictures, but he'd worried all the time and wasn't about to leave now.

He kept his eyes on his closet. Without looking at the next bed, "You want anything?"

"No." Elephant Ears had one leg.

He wasn't worried about the staff looking in there, but he was always finding some oatmeal head wandering around with his slippers or underwear. You couldn't put anything down. He'd have to come up with some other hiding place for the future, but right now just let someone try to get in there. Just let them try.

At ten minutes to eleven he was crouched by her car. The doors weren't locked, as he had feared. He slid into the back, closing the door as noiselessly as he could, and stayed low against the floor.

He was trembling violently. For some reason, he thought of the first time he'd watched someone go to the chair. He was nervous then, too, especially when he had heard the approaching screams, but a kind of calm had come over him as he thought of that young girl, her stomach slashed open. And after that he'd watched every bum go he put in the chair. Eight of them. Seven? Not that he liked seeing it. Hell no. But if you're gonna put someone in the chair, be there.

Remembering that calmed him, too, and like something filling a vacuum the full flood of his rage was back. Now he could hear some crinkly sounds around him, footsteps on the pebbly asphalt, then here and there the sound of a motor as the three-to-eleven shift was leaving. Then the door on the driver's side opened and finally closed.

"See you tomorrow, Joannie," the driver called out.

"See you. Big doings tonight?"

"Yeah," followed by fake snoring and a laugh. Now the motor roared. He got a whiff of cigarette smoke and made a face and had to fight against coughing. They were starting to move.

He didn't wait long, just for about a block. He rose up and sat on the back seat and as he did he said, "Just keep driving, do what I say."

There was a gasp and she turned, saw the gun, that round face, the glasses. "Oh, my God."

"In that driveway. Over there. There!"

"Oh, my God."

She turned in. The driveway led to an abandoned warehouse in the middle of a couple acres of broken paving and a scattering of brush and trees.

"Stop the car."

She did. She turned again. "Please. Pl—"

He shot her squarely in the face.

He got out quickly, afraid blood would spurt on him. She was thrashing from side to side, silently, her face gushing blood, then crumbled over, twisted, against the back of the seat, part of her face toward him. He was trembling again as he watched her. She'd stopped moving. He reached in gingerly and touched her head with the revolver, then drew back a little, and even though she hadn't stirred he fired again, this time at the top of her head, and fought the urge to reach the full satisfaction of just emptying the whole goddamn barrel in her.

He started to leave but then remembered, and with his coat he wiped off the handles of the door he used. He trudged up the drive, but instead of going directly out to the street he paralleled it along the warehouse grounds. Now he would have to go out to the street for a block, then cross another street to go up the driveway to the home. He stepped out to the sidewalk and walked as casually as he could. Tonight, unlike last night, he was wearing street clothes under his coat.

The houses, as he remembered from the bus ride they'd taken to that fucken orchard, were set far apart here. An occasional car was parked for the night along the curb. It was a quiet street, but the street fronting the grounds of the home was usually fairly busy, at least during the day, and as he came close to it he felt as though his calves had turned to rocks. It had become painful to walk.

He saw an occasional car go past the intersection ahead. Now, at the corner, he had to stop for a while because of the pain. A flash of memory made him connect it with fear. He'd had his moments of fear, sometimes drawing him at the groin and a sensation going down his legs, though he'd never told Josie that, God rest her soul, nor anyone else for that matter. Somehow the memory loosened his calves a little; and seeing headlights in the distance, little dots, he walked across the street and then straight on past the entrance.

When the car passed he turned back and walked up the drive, then cut across the lawn, which was nice and dark, to where it was a relatively short walk across to the side of the building. At the door he had a frightening few moments trying to unlock it, but it gave. He locked it from the inside, pocketed the key, then sagged fullweight against a wall, breathing heavily. A peek from the storeroom found the alcove to be clear, but another one from there took in a nurse standing in the hall. He slipped back into the storeroom. He waited a few minutes, then stepped into the alcove again. She was putting something away in a closet, her back to him. He stepped quickly across the hall to his room, stood there in the dark, not knowing if she heard or saw, if she was coming. A glance to the side told him Elephant Ears was still asleep.

He walked to his bed, got undressed as quickly as he could; his coat fell from the hook in the closet but he was in too much of a hurry to pick it up, just closed the door on it. He took out the pillow and extra blanket he'd bunched under the cover, and slipped in and lay there, gasping, lungs burning. Soon he felt himself slowing down, then fully at peace. He'd forgotten how it felt to be free of rage.

3

Some youngsters who went to the warehouse grounds to play found the body the following afternoon. Various cards in her handbag identified her to the police as Kay Latimore, forty-two, who lived about four miles away and worked over at the Linwood Convalescent Home. Since she was in uniform she obviously was on her way to or from work. Her handbag or clothing didn't seem disturbed, so unless the killer had been frightened away the motive clearly hadn't been robbery or rape. Since the warehouse was set off a good distance from any houses, it seemed unlikely that anything would have scared off the killer. It looked like an out-and-out assassination.

The officers broke into three teams, one going to her house, another to scour the neighborhood around the scene, the third to the nursing home. At her home they found that she was a widow who lived with her sister and had a recently married daughter. She was dating a widower, but a quick check established that he was out of town and had been for the past three days. Neither her grief-crushed sister nor neighbors could think of any reason for the murder. The word just about everyone used to describe her was "good." A good person. A good soul. A good nurse.

The canvass of the homes near the warehouse, meanwhile, was

coming up with nothing so far. No one had heard a shot, seen any suspicious persons or cars.

At the nursing home, here again the word they heard over and over was "good." As the administrator, a man named Cummings, said, "That's the only way you can describe her."

Detective Lieutenant LaSala, of Homicide, and one of his men and two precinct men were with Cummings and the director of nurses, Doris Doral, in Cummings' office.

"Forgetting about *enemies*, she didn't have anyone who... as much as didn't like her?" LaSala asked.

"I'm telling you, I can't think of one person, *one* person, ever speaking against her," Mrs. Doral said, her eyes red and watery.

"Not even any of the patients?"

"You can't count *them.* Have you seen them? Walk around and see."

"Actually, I meant their families. Did any of them have a quarrel with her over anything? Have anything against her?"

"No. Certainly not that I know of. Of course, we all get complaints that Dad has a cold or why is Mom in restraints. It's not to say that's all we get, but we do get them."

One of the precinct men said, "Would the complaints come to the office?"

"You mean instead of to the floor nurse?" Cummings asked. "Both. If they have any serious complaint I'm sure they would complain to the office. But sometimes they'll just say something to the nurse or whoever's on the floor."

"Were there any recently involving Mrs. Latimore's patients?"

"I really can't think of anything offhand."

Mrs. Doral said, "If anyone did complain to Kay she would have marked it down in her notes in the patient's chart. We insist on that. And if it was anything serious, she would also make out what we call an Incident Report and send it to the office."

"Is there any chance she wouldn't have? I mean, you know, not to look bad?"

"Anything, of course, is possible. But, number one, I can't see Kay ever doing that. Two, it's risky. The family that complains to her might complain to someone else also, to the office, and then we find it's not on her chart or we don't have a record of it."

"We'll want to look at her charts and your records," said LaSala. "Now, we've been talking about recently. What about not-so-recently? Can you remember any big hassle?"

"That's asking a lot. Kay was here nine years," Cummings said.

"Let's say this past year."

"Nothing stands out in my mind. But look, we'll try to think."

"What about anyone who might have liked her too much? Do you know of any employees, for instance, she might have turned down for a date?"

Neither of them did.

"When's the last time you saw her?"

Cummings hadn't seen her at all yesterday, but Mrs. Doral had spoken with her in the office about four in the afternoon.

"Did she seem concerned about anything?"

"Not at all."

"What did she talk about?"

"She stopped in to show me her son-in-law's picture, and she talked about what a nice apartment they had."

"You weren't on when she left for the night?"

"No, I left at five-thirty. I don't take a regular shift."

To Cummings, "Do you own the home?"

"No, it's part of a chain. Headquarters are on the West Coast."

The officers wanted to know more about the home, and he explained that it had a hundred and twenty beds, all of which were presently occupied. The home had a contract with the government to take care of Veterans Administration patients, so that was thirty-two beds right there. Many of the other patients were there under Medicare, but after that ran out they either left or became private pay. The home, he said with a certain pride, did not take any Medicaid, any welfare patients.

"How many employees do you have?" LaSala asked.

"Well, I'll have to check to give you the exact amount," Cummings said, "but there are twenty nurses, thirty-six aides and orderlies, about fifteen people in the kitchen. Then, we have maintenance people, housekeeping, laundry. Oh, the physical therapist, a hairdresser who comes in, a podiatrist comes in. I'll give you the list."

"What about physicians? You didn't mention physicians."

"My head. This thing's really got me. We have a medical director who serves as house doctor, and three other house doctors. None of them are here full time. They have their own practices. The residents are also permitted to use their own doctors if they want."

The three-to-eleven shift, Kay Latimore's, had come on about ten minutes ago, and LaSala went to Wing B while the others started questioning staff on the other wings. He learned nothing new there, other than that Dr. Bennett had stopped in about a quarter to six and stayed a half hour. Also, three of the patients had had visitors after dinner, all of whom would have left at nine at the latest. LaSala jotted down Bennett's office and home phone numbers and, after conferring with the nurses and the office, found out who the visitors were. They would question all of them, of course, as well as members of the eleven-to-seven shift, which had replaced the murdered woman's.

As he was walking to join the others he threaded his way carefully around several patients in wheelchairs or using walkers. After almost thirty years of being a cop, and seeing every horror in the book, no way anything here could bother him. But suddenly he paused by the main lounge, where a number of patients were sitting, many in wheelchairs, a couple of them now and then glancing at the darkened TV. His face grew pained. Although it was years since he had seen the captain, the old man hadn't changed all that much that he couldn't recognize him. He was sitting by the picture window, looking out at the garden, wearing a heavy buttondown sweater despite its being very comfortable in the home, and trousers that looked like they hadn't been pressed in a year, and his shoes were sort of scruffy. He remembered the captain as so natty, a big man brightly bald and always hatless. Even when you'd see a glimpse of the long underwear he wore on some of those all-night stakeouts, you'd see a perfectly white line, and somehow the underwear never even crumpled his socks.

He felt an emptiness in his chest as he stood wondering should he go over. He'd heard that his wife died a couple of years ago, and then that he was living in Florida—no, with one of his children. Had no idea he was in a nursing home. Uneasily, he walked over.

He tried sounding cheerful. "How you doing, Captain?"

The captain slowly looked up at him. He didn't seem to recognize him.

"LaSala, Captain. Nick LaSala. Remember—your squad?" He tried thinking of something that would jog his memory. "Broke a toe kicking in a cellar door that time?" He couldn't be sure if there was any recognition, but there seemed to be.

He kneeled next to him. "Hey, you're looking good. Real good."

He was standing up slowly now, trying to hold back a grimace. Then he began walking away.

Mother of God, is that what happens to you? A nice place, a real nice place, but still is this what happens to you? There was a guy that had, what, a hundred and fifty official commendations? At least that. There was the greatest cop that ever walked this living earth. No Sherlock Holmes, but a cop, a real cop. You couldn't even begin to count the busts. And to be on his squad, Christ, to be on his squad was the greatest honor you could have, though the guys who never made it were so jealous: all he's after is the headlines! He got the headlines all right, but because he broke more cases than anyone.

They called it the General Crimes Squad. It was a special squad made up of about twenty-five guys. Except for the captain, none of them were detectives. Plainclothesmen. No hoity-toity detectives, but cops who'd been on the streets and knew the beats and the hoods and had the wires. Sometimes, though, the captain took on a kid, like himself. He was tapped right from the academy because the pushers didn't know his face yet, and they dropped him into the streets, into that rathole of a barroom. But none of the pushers would touch him until the captain set him up that time in the bar, walked down the length of it as he and the boys often did, just to see who was new in town, then suddenly grabbed him by the collar and shook him and slapped him once, good, across the face because he'd lifted his arms—"You stay clean, bum, you hear me? You stay clean!" After that, maybe a day or two, the pushers started coming out of their holes to him.

But junk was only part of it. The squad was called in whenever there was a specially tough case, a murder, a bank job, whatever, which was why Homicide and all the other squads and the precinct boys would get so hot at them—because this was a squad that crossed lines. Yes, even a county line or two. LaSala almost smiled as he thought of the time the captain raced them into Parkmont County to swoop up Bevin because Parkmont was playing around with it, waiting for more evidence, and he had a hunch Bevin was the salesman's killer, and like most of his hunches it was a good one. Maybe you couldn't get away with it these days—not that they'd admitted to where they'd picked him up—but those days the lawyers could yell all they wanted, they had Bevin and the confession.

They used to say, too, some people, that the captain had the key to the mint because he knew all the bookies and could occasionally close his eyes. LaSala didn't know about that, and if so, so what. God help the guy, whoever he was, who made a victim. If you made a victim, whether through murder or a hustle, God watch over you. Oh, could the captain be tough! Oh, boy. Once he'd knocked this heavyweight contender who'd killed his wife clear across a room, and the guy just lay there, his eyeballs rolled back. But he could be soft, too. The fact is, no one in the force outside his boys had the slightest idea how many ex-cons and their families he helped. Once he settled the score, and you showed you were trying, nothing he wouldn't do for you.

But Jesus, *now*.

LaSala cleared his throat as he thought of the captain sitting there, closing his eyes, then the dark widening stain that appeared on his trousers.

He waited several minutes before opening his eyes. His pulse was racing. It was hard, still, to settle down.

He looked down at his trousers. Could have held it in. *Had to get rid of him.*

Somehow he'd never thought about cops coming here.

He was embarrassed and held a magazine over his crotch as he made his way back to his room. It made him look especially feeble. He passed several nurses and aides who were crying.

It was about time they cried, those bastards!

Those fucks, it was a lesson they'd better remember.

4

As he always did on his early morning three-mile jog, David Bennett sprinted the last block to his home. He stood partly bent over by the front door now, breathing through his mouth, then straightened up and whipped off his headband and took another long deep breath before going into the house. His heart was still hammering away as he walked up to the second floor, but it was settling down as he tested the shower with his hand before stepping into the stall.

When he had first started jogging three years ago it was half with the fear that his heart would take one big final pound and then burst. But he had long stopped thinking about that, had finally come to believe what he used to tell so many of his coronaries when they told him they were afraid they would drop dead having sex or climbing a flight of stairs or even going to the corner store for a paper. With a gradual build-up of exercise, with a lot of the stress off and, Christ, without all those cigarettes, his heart was stronger than ever. Well, maybe not stronger than ever, but certainly stronger than those last few months before the attack.

After a good, relaxing shower and a brisk rubdown with a thick towel, he came out naked to the bedroom. Laura had gotten up and nodded to him with a yawn as she worked her arms through her robe.

She went into the bathroom while he got dressed, and by the time she came downstairs he'd had orange juice and was settling down with coffee and toast and the paper open to the sports section. He looked up long enough to ask how she slept and she said fine, you? And he said fine too, and she took part of the paper and they both remained absorbed for a while until she mentioned that she was getting in that new line of dresses from Italy.

"Great. I told you not to worry."

"I hope we're doing the right thing. They're super-expensive."

"First you worry you're not going to get them, now that maybe you shouldn't have."

"I think we'll do all right with them."

She and a girl friend had opened a small shop six years ago, a few months after the younger of their two children had gone off to college. She turned out to be an excellent businesswoman, could expand the business greatly if she wanted to, but she wanted it the way it was, something to do, something that made a little money and she had fun with. And she was still very much involved with golf—she had the fifth lowest handicap among the women at the club—though her interest had sagged when some new women joined and dropped her from first. That had started her smoking again, but she was losing the big can she'd started to develop—that she *always* developed when she was down—and was almost slender again.

She was in the bathroom again when he left. "Leaving," he called from the steps. "Take it easy."

"You too."

He pulled into his spot in the parking lot of Creighton Instruments, Inc. at five of nine and was in his clinic on the seventh floor at exactly two minutes after nine. Mrs. Reynolds was already taking a blood pressure—he had never seen the fellow before so it was most likely a preemployment physical—and Rosa was taking the cover off her typewriter at her desk right outside his office. Mrs. Reynolds, whom he rarely saw without that filmy little cupcake of a cap, and who still talked with some pride of the old days when nurses wouldn't dare wear pantsuits, acknowledged him with a slight nod. Rosa, who was three months pregnant and whom he hated to lose, said, "Good morning, Dr. Bennett."

"How's it going?"

"I've stopped throwing up," she said while he was standing over his desk, leafing through the mail in his in-box. It usually didn't come this early.

"Didn't I say?" he said without looking up.

After putting on a freshly laundered lab jacket, he came back to his desk and settled down with the mail and numerous interoffice memos, ending up at length with a monthly newspaper for industrial physicians. He had come to work at Creighton seven years ago, a little less than a year after his coronary, which had happened shortly after his fortieth birthday—something a psychiatrist could make a lot of. In fact, one had. He'd been so down he had seen a shrink a few times after he came home from the hospital, and the shrink had tried to get him to talk about forty, what it meant to him, but the truth—or at least the truth as he saw it then—was that forty was just another year. He had never really given forty a thought, which had the shrink talking about denial. Anyway, he knew what caused it. The big thing was the stress, and add smoking to that and you don't need to know much else. He'd had a general practice and, unlike a lot of the fellows, had given too much of himself to too many people. It was that . . . and other things. But that certainly had to go.

"David, it could be a good idea," the shrink had said, "and if that's what you want to do you ought to give thought to doing it. But the only thing I'm concerned about, and that you should think about, is if you're trying to run away from a problem. You can't run away from emotional problems."

This, when David brought up the possibility of giving up private practice.

Well, you don't have to be a shrink to know you can't run away from emotional problems. The fact is, you can lower realistic pressures. And there were almost none here and, compared with general practice, very little at the nursing home. Here, you might have to patch someone up who welded his finger instead of a piece of a computer, or try to keep a heart going until an ambulance got here. There were the preemployments, of course, and an occasional appendix, and flu shots, and menstrual cramps, and all the educational programs and the alcoholism program that was so successful.

The nursing home, which brought his income up to what he'd been making before, helped keep his hand in medicine without its being a real strain. He just wouldn't let it. He would do everything medically possible for those people; but he couldn't make them young again or uncork the arteries to their brains or keep them from eventually dying or reunite them with mates or children who didn't want them or couldn't handle them or were dead. He listened to them and their families, treated them kindly, of course, but knew when to turn off when they began unloading the impossible on him. If he had learned anything in the coronary care unit, with the tubes and the monitors, it was the price of being too emotionally involved.

Strange, how he rarely thought of the coronary care unit anymore. But whenever he did, it was almost always with a mixture of anger and embarrassment. The first time Laura walked in he said quietly, but obviously loud enough to cause some of the nurses to turn, "Get out of here." She looked like she'd been shot, and she sat down, just staring at him wide-eyed, and that's when he yelled it out—"Get *out* of here!" One of the nurses led her out then, and she wasn't let back in until the next day, after he asked for her. When she sat by him he squeezed her hand and his eyes filled up.

But the anger had been real and didn't fully go away. It was, as he'd analyzed it, a whole swirl of things, some of it true, some of it bullshit, just plain *blaming*. At times he couldn't separate them, distinguish one from the other. Like having the babies so soon. He had been in the last year of medical school and she was a lab technician when they had married, and of course she would keep working while he finished his internship and residency in surgery. But the second week of internship she was pregnant with Karen.

All right, that was old stuff. Later, over all the years, had she ever once said, "David, why don't you take it easy?" As far as he could remember the only times she came close was when a housecall or emergency made them late for a party.

She hadn't even believed that he was having a coronary. He hadn't had the typical pains—it had been a mild one, really—but he had a sick feeling he recognized, the feeling of *blaah,* where all you want to do is lie down, and then there was the chilly sweat and slight nausea.

He'd said, "Laura, I think I'm having a coronary."

"Oh, come on." She seemed annoyed, as she always did when he complained.

A bunch of things like that.

But it was *all* bullshit. And he shut it from his mind.

At about eleven o'clock that morning he got a call from a detective whose name he didn't catch. The detective simply said he'd like to talk to him and was checking to see if he was in. About a half hour later a Homicide detective named Goldner was sitting in his office, telling him of the murder.

"We understand you were in last night and spoke to her. We thought maybe she said something that could help us."

"I just don't believe this." It must have been the second or third time he said it.

"You can believe it all right. Did she seem worried about anything?"

"No, not at all."

"Is there anything you can tell us about her that might help? Did she have any enemies you know of? Any boy friend in the place?"

"If she did I don't know about it. I'm really knocked for a loop."

"Well, if you think of anything you'll let us know, of course."

"Oh Christ, yes."

Goldner gone, he was sitting at his desk with a look of anguish. Who would kill her? Why? The fact was he didn't really know her. Know her as a person, that is. Only now was she coming to life for him. He knew her as a super-efficient nurse, someone who could find the tiniest dried-up vein for an IV, never screwed up a catheterization, could get hip fractures on their feet sooner than any other nurse, was relentless when it came to trying to prevent decubiti; someone you could really trust with an order.

Oh, Christ, what a hell of a world.

He felt drained, all hollowed-out.

He found himself thinking of the fantasies he'd been having occasionally since his talk with Pat Andreoli last week in the office near her station, after she'd cried herself out. What if he'd really been screwing her, and *she* had been killed, and the police asked him if she had any boy friends in the place?

For several moments he felt anxious, as though it had really happened.

5

The captain woke the next morning from a deep sleep, feeling exceptionally good until, like someone remembering he's got to undergo surgery that day, he felt a throbbing flush of anxiety as he thought about the gun and bullets in his closet. Had to hide 'em, but where? He had looked up and down the halls and in various rooms yesterday but couldn't find a place he could trust. And he couldn't just sit here most of the day guarding them.

"Good morning, Captain, good morning, Mr. Silverstein," an aide sang out. The captain watched as she set Elephant Ears' breakfast in front of him. "We're going to get you in a wheelchair today, Mr. Silverstein. Isn't that great?" Elephant Ears kept flopping his toothless, lip-heavy mouth as he stared at the food. "Time for breakfast, Captain," she said. "Come on, breakfast."

He waited until she left the room before he went into the bathroom and brushed his teeth—he'd had only four cavities in his whole life—and flapped some water on his face and dried himself off, thinking. He began to get dressed slowly. After putting on his trousers he also put on a suit jacket, though it was to a different pair of pants, and then put the gun with all its plastic wrapping in one of the jacket's side pockets and the box of cartridges in the left pants pocket.

But the jacket bulged and hung down on the gun side. He looked at his topcoat in the closet, then, after several moments' reflection, put it on. He looked like a nut, he thought. So? They were all nut-o's here.

He walked down the hall, deliberately crouching slightly, sensing it went along with the coat.

"Uncle Josh! I'm gonna get good marks, Uncle Josh. I'm a good girl."

He was almost used to hearing such wails from the rooms, but when he heard someone in back of him say, "Goopy, goopy, goopy," he started to turn in anger until he remembered the guy who always said, "Goopy, goopy, goopy."

"Keep hitting 'em, Beeno," he said without looking back. Beeno—a name he just made up—liked to hit. He was tied into a wheelchair.

The captain walked on. In the dining room, which was warmly decorated and furnished in Colonial style, he walked over to one of the empty round tables. Someone came up from behind him, probably a nurse, and said, "Are you cold, Captain?" and put her hand firmly on his forehead. He pushed it away.

"Aren't we being nasty today?" and she put her hand firmly on his forehead again. He let it stay there, closing his eyes. The rod, he thought, feels like it's going to fall out; it was weighing down his coat. He wondered what he'd do if it did fall out. Go for it? He'd go for it. He could see himself holding it straight out with both hands as he backed away toward the front door. He would hate to kill a pedestrian, though. The times he'd fired from a car or running after a guy there were never any pedestrians.

"You're fine," she was saying. "I'm going to check the air conditioner."

He only had some prune juice and a cup of Sanka and a half a slice of dry toast. He was anxious to get on with it. He walked out to the veranda to think things out, the chairs empty behind him as he stood facing the grounds from the railing. Then he walked down the few steps and started inspecting the grounds, the sides of the building, looking at the big slop buckets in back, the pile of old rainspouts they were saving for some reason, then over to the other side of the building where they kept some rabbits behind wiring. He looked at the hutch, wondering if he could hide it there, but it seemed too conspicuous. He was getting desperate and toured the grounds again, looking at the trees for some kind of hole or covered spot. Then, though he'd passed this before without thinking about it, he stared at the mound of firewood left over from the winter. He walked over to it, then glanced around and tentatively pushed a log down. He pulled at a few others until he had an opening. Quickly he shoved in the gun and cartridges, making sure they were totally in the plastic. Then he lifted a log and put it back in place and, though they were heavier, two others.

There. He stood away from the mound, breathing hard, sensing a little ache in his right shoulder. He counted the number of logs that covered it from the top. Three. Had to remember this. Three. His thumb, the next finger and the other. He'd keep the rod there until he could find someplace better.

Meanwhile, the thumb, the next finger and the other.

He started walking away, feeling relaxed now. He had always felt better knowing the gun was nearby. After he learned they were retiring him and he asked them if he could keep his gun and they told him it was against regs, which he knew—but if anyone deserved his gun it was him—well, after that, when he was on his second from the last job, and there was this cache of rods, he just lifted one. A .38 Smith & Wesley—Smith & Wesson. And after Josie died, God rest her soul, and Ellen insisted he live with her, he took the gun along. And he took it to Rosemarie's later, and to Mark's, and back and forth again until one day Rosemarie said she was going to get rid of it, she wasn't going to keep no gun in the house with the kids. He pleaded with her but she said there was no talking about it, and he finally thought of the doghouse and told her about this friend of his he gave it to. She was suspicious at first when he couldn't remember the name and she tore the house apart a few times, and then grumbled something or other and never asked again. He'd hated to see the kids mad at him; that always made him feel so bad. He never wanted to be a pain in the ass to anyone, and he had begged them to let him live on his own in the first place, he'd been on his own since he was fifteen, but they wouldn't let him because once, maybe *twice,* he'd locked himself out of the house. Who the hell never locked himself out of the house?

But there was Ellen saying over and over, "Who's going to take care of you if something happens?" until he really got scared. It was good at Ellen's and he liked being there. He tried to stay out of the way, and it even felt good to know that Rosemarie wanted him, and Mark, too. But soon, even though you couldn't help knowing you were a pain in the ass, you were stuck, you were *afraid* to be on your own now. And all the time you felt so guilty when you did something stupid, like that time at Rosemarie's when he woke in the middle of the night and thought it was the night before and he was still at Mark's, and he got out of bed and took a right in the dark, because he didn't want to turn on the lights and wake anyone, and went to the bathroom next door—only next door was a bedroom at Rosemarie's and there like an asshole he took a piss on the floor.

It was the first time he'd ever cried in front of any of his kids, but Rosemarie said now, now, it's all right, but there was that roll of her eyes when she went for a bucket. But she and Lou kept him, and when he had to go in for the operation they said his bed would be right there waiting for him, and they said it again when they brought him here to recuperate. And here, looking around, wanting to run, surrounded on every side by slobbering horrors and tubes up the nose and in the arms and pricks and people with bags of amber urine strapped to them, he used to go on his knees every night, "Dear God, dear Jesus, dear Josie who's looking over me, thank you for my children, my great wonderful children." But then one day the three of them came at the same time, which in itself was unusual, and after a while Mark showed him the framed photo of Josie and himself at that mountain resort, which he always kept with him, and Mark was saying, "You should keep this in your apartment."

Slowly: "What apartment?"

"Here. Your apartment."

"This," and he was shaking his head, "ain't an apartment."

"Well, it's a real nice room," Rosemarie said. "Hey, look what I brought you from the children," and she started rooting in her bag.

"I want to go home." Even now he could remember the exact swelling of fear.

"Papa, don't do this," Ellen said, tears in her eyes. And Mark was looking away, but Rosemarie, who was always the toughest, came up with some shit from her bag and said, "Kenny and Lucy made these for you. They said, 'We want grandpop to have them.'"

Mark said, "Look, Dad, you're better off here. It's a beautiful place and these people are trained to take care of you."

And that's when he said what he shouldn't, when he used that word. "All of you—get the fuck out of here! Get the fuck out of my sight!"

He must have screamed the words because people were suddenly all around him, he could hear all kinds of voices. He couldn't remember it but they must have given him a needle because the next he knew he was undressed in bed and it was the middle of the night.

They took turns visiting him every couple of weeks, but he wouldn't as much as go for a ride with them or give them the satisfaction of saying much more than yes or no to them.

"Well, Captain," an aide was saying to him now, "I see you've taken off your coat."

And he was walking straighter.

The captain didn't see LaSala come back that day but he was quite aware that a few guys with the definite look of cop about them were wandering about, talking to people here and there. He spent most of the day in one of the lounges, the one near the front door, watching TV; but his gaze occasionally drifted over to see where they were. He saw the last of them leave early in the afternoon.

He didn't really give much thought to Kay Latimore until three-to-eleven came on, and he saw that Garbo was taking Latimore's place at the station today. She usually worked mornings, seven-to-three; and though he couldn't remember what the real Garbo looked like, it seemed to him she had sandylike hair, and the name just popped into mind. Her name was something like Annie Oly, not that he gave a goddamn, they were all no good, they all turned on you. She acted sweetie sweetie, but just wait, she would turn.

Latimore, though, was a name you didn't forget. "Be a good boy for Latimore." Or, "Rosie, keep in those teeth, this is Latimore." And all that crap about "state." If you didn't do this or that you were going off to "state."

Once in a while she said the whole thing, "state hospital."

Poor old Missy. Wrinkled, wacky. Stockings always down around her ankles.

"Harry," and she'd tugged at him.

"I ain't Harry, lady," he used to say.

Once he let her hold his hand. He remembered her smile and the way she put her bony little fingers between his. But he never let her go for the pecker.

He didn't mind that Elephant Ears did, though. He used to turn to the other side in bed and didn't look or have one bad thought even though he heard sounds. No, once he did look, but all she was doing was playing with it. He couldn't care less what they did. Like the girls. Oh, he pulled them in when he had to but he always treated them nice as long as they weren't rolling anyone, as long as there weren't complaints. Some of the nicest people he ever knew were working whores, though he himself never touched one. Oh, one. Two maybe.

But then one evening Latimore came in with all that crap to poor old frightened Missy about state, about seeing to it that Dr. Benny sent her to state.

He'd said, "What do you want to do that for? Let her alone."

"Stay out of this. You're no innocent, either, mister. You ought to be ashamed of yourself."

"Let her alone."

But the next day there was poor old Missy in one of those goddamn chairs all tied up, crying, rocking back and forth. "Let her go." "Soon, Captain. Now run along, everything will be fine." Then, the following morning, gone. And she, all in white like some fucken angel, going right on with her life. Oh, and how are we today? That bastard, that bastard!

Even now his temples pounded at the thought of her, the way they'd pounded those days in court when he thought Hattie Mooney might just get life, when her lawyer talked about church this and church that, all her fucken good work, like somehow that should make you forget those two poor slobs she got through the lovelorn columns and then hacked and robbed and buried out near the pigs.

You had no right to take a human life. And Missy's was a life. She had friends here and used to smile here and wasn't frightened here.

Hattie Mooney, say hello to Latimore.

That's what he'd thought when he had suddenly remembered the gun in the doghouse. And that one thought was better than a whole bottle of aspirin: it took away the headache he'd had ever since he'd seen Missy tied.

He couldn't close the case completely, though, until Dr. Benny went, too. But that would have to wait until things calmed down.

6

He picked up the phone at Rosa's buzz. "Dr. Bennett, a Mr. Diamond is on the phone. He's calling from Illinois. He's with Lyke Pharmaceuticals."

He pushed the button on the phone and said, "This is Dr. Bennett."

Diamond introduced himself as assistant manager of the general promotion department. "I just read your article in *Physician's View.* I want you to know how much I like it."

"Well, that's very nice of you. Thank you."

"As you probably know, doctor, we send out a great deal of material to physicians as part of our continuing education services. And we'd like to reprint your article in one of our publications, the *Lyke Reporter.* Now, we've spoken to *Physician's View* and it's fine with them but they said, of course, that we need your permission. Now if you do agree to it, and I certainly hope you will, we'll pay an honorarium of two hundred and fifty dollars."

"All right, that sounds fine."

"Great. I'll write you a letter today confirming it. Incidentally, I just happened to think of it, we'll need your picture. A black and white glossy, a head shot. If you don't happen to have one we'll pay for having one made."

"I think I have one. I'll check."

"Fine. By the way, doctor, we have a great many educational projects going on here, we have a deep commitment to the elderly. I imagine you've seen some of our booklets, films, our tape cassettes. What I'm saying is would it be all right if I call on you in the future to discuss some other projects?"

"I'll be more than glad to discuss whatever you have in mind."

"Good. I'll be in touch. And thanks again."

Hanging up, David sat at his desk for a few moments more, thinking of the conversation. He felt quite good about it, though he wasn't fooling himself why they wanted the article. It was no great piece—indeed, it had been turned down by the prestigious journals such as *JAMA* and the *New England Journal of Medicine.* It consisted basically of the case histories of three patients at the home who had "restless leg syndrome." It was a problem many elderly people complained of—their legs felt tired, achy, and restless when they lay in bed at night—and there was no known cause or any established treatment for it. He had found in those three cases that the new tranquilizer Darlonex gave longer remissions than any other medication he'd tried. Lyke Pharmaceuticals, of course, made Darlonex.

Still, he was quite pleased. It was the first paper he had written in years.

At six-thirty that evening he stopped at the home for the bimonthly Patient Care Policy Meeting. Rukkenmeyer, the medical director—like himself, an industrial physician—was there, as were Kliegman, an osteopath two years in practice, and Cummings the administrator, and Doral the director of nurses. David was annoyed that the other doctor on the staff didn't show up—he didn't believe a word of his excuse—but his annoyance was mostly at himself because he had given up tennis for this, could have switched the meeting.

But the meeting didn't last long. They discussed their infection control procedures and then, before breaking up, David said they should have more water mattresses on hand for patients with decubiti. Cummings felt this was an unnecessary expense for the few times they might need them all, but Rukkenmeyer then settled it with a brusk, "Dr. Bennett's absolutely right. Look, either this is a fine home or it isn't. And if it isn't, I don't want any part of it."

Soon after David left the conference room he saw a nurse and aide walking across the lobby toward the entrance to Wing B.

"Miss Andreoli."

She turned, came back, while the aide walked on.

He said, "Since when are you working three-to-eleven?"

"I'm taking Kay's place until they get someone else."

"Oh. God, what a nightmare."

"It's so hard to believe. I still see her right in front of me."

"Have you heard anything?"

"No. You?"

"No, except they think maybe it could be someone from here because it happened so close. Maybe someone followed her. But they also don't know if it could be someone who was waiting for her or maybe someone she gave a ride to."

"She'd never pick up anyone she didn't know. But who knows? But I can't believe it could be someone from here. I'm so gloomy, I'm so depressed. And I'm going to tell you, I'm a little scared." She took a deep breath. "Anyway, I want to thank you again."

"There's no reason to thank me. I didn't really do anything."

"Thanks," and she nodded with a little smile. "Well, I have to go back. Good night."

"Take it easy."

He watched her walk off: tall, slender, fine nose and cheekbones, and just a trace of perfume lingering behind. Then he wondered if he should make rounds as long as he was here. No. Why go looking for trouble?

By the time Pat Andreoli reached the nursing station she admitted to herself that she envied his wife, whoever she was. It had nothing to do with his looks, though he was quite good-looking, with a strong, angular face and black, graying hair. Nor was it that he was a doctor. She wasn't all that big on doctors. In fact, she could probably count on her hand how many doctors she really respected for dedication, humanness, fully knowing their stuff. And though he obviously knew his medicine, she wasn't sure where he fit in. Certainly, at least from what she could see here, not one of the great ones. With him, as with most of the others here, it was in and out—do everything you had to, but no lingering. But not one of the shits either. A shit would have made her feel foolish crying over the death of an old man, but he had sat with her in the office and waited until she cried herself out, and afterward had said what made sense: "You've got to stop feeling so much. Otherwise you won't have any more of yourself to give."

Not that he was completely right. Not at all. But he hadn't put her down.

The honest-to-God reason she envied his wife was that she was married to a solid guy. Or maybe married, period.

No, not married, period. She could still have been married to Warren. As it was, with his drinking and those terrible times when he actually hit her, afterward crying and pleading to give him another chance, how in God's name had she put up with him for five years? And all the cu-reeps she'd met up with since. How could one person meet so many creeps?

Well. Enough of that self-pity, Patricia.

Let's see who needs what.

She made medication rounds of the rooms with an aide. Mr. Buckley, a harmless burned-out schizo, said, "Was you me today?"

"No, I wasn't you today, Mr. Buckley. *You're* you."

"Me me?"

"Sure, you're you. That's a handsome shirt you got on there. Who bought it, your daughter?"

"Dor."

"Right. Your daughter."

Out in the hall, Mrs. Granley, a grand lady if there ever was one, said, "You know, I haven't heard from my husband since he died." She was crying.

"Come on, darling, walk with us. Would you like to walk with us?"

The captain, she saw, didn't want to talk, so she didn't press, just waited there until he swallowed his pill. "Mr. Silverstein, how does it feel being in a wheelchair?"

"Yuh."

"As soon as you're stronger you'll be going everywhere by yourself."

Dr. Persky, a wizened little man in a geriatric chair, said, "Hello, doll. I say thank you. I say thank you for realizing I still have my marbles. I am not cuckoo. I get depressed something terrible, but I am not cuckoo. They can drive you cuckoo here. You talk to them, you say, 'Give me another cigar,' they won't look at you. It can get terribly depressing. One day you're a surgeon, next day you're a patient. I thank you for talking to me."

"It's a pleasure talking to you."

"That's a very good expression. That makes a person feel good. I was a toosie doctor. You know what a toosie doctor is? It is my own expression. I cut out hemorrhoids. I worked with the toosie but I never forgot a patient had a mouth. I always talked to a patient. I treated them like human beings, not toosies."

"You were a very wise, kind person."

"That's another very good expression. Thank you, doll."

Other nurses, she reflected as she walked on, often asked her, "How do you work with them all the time?" She just *liked* to. They couldn't seem to understand that. Oh, once in a while it did get her down terribly. For some reason or another, she would feel particularly close to certain patients, and when they died it really hurt. Maybe there was a special bravery they showed, or maybe they reminded you of someone, but even though they were old and sick, and often in so much pain they were better off dead, and you even wished death for them—still, it hurt and you ached when it happened. She didn't go around bawling all the time, but sometimes you couldn't help feeling something to the core of your heart.

Now, back at the station, she started on some paperwork, only to stop soon. She had begun thinking of Kay again and it was as though a poker had entered her chest. What made it worse was that she couldn't deny that sometimes she didn't particularly like her, or that Kay could be just too cold at times. Nor did she quite like herself for thinking only in terms of herself now. Though it was only a little before eight, she was already dreading eleven o'clock, walking out to the parking lot. But she was sure everyone would walk out together, would look out for each other.

The captain never thought of it, but if he had he would have realized that he had not had a conversation with anyone since he had come to the home, particularly from the time he learned he was to stay. He would say a few words here and there, but most of the time he just wandered about or slept or read a little or watched TV, mostly without interest. When someone came up to him and talked craziness, he was sarcastic, as though it was a shield that would keep him from being infected with their craziness. Like Punchie saying all the time, "Was you me today?" "Yeah, and I killed myself." And he would avoid whoever did make sense, as though talking to them would be a kind of giving in.

He tried not to think of past good times, either; but that was hard. So he would think of the beach house he and Josie, God rest her soul, would take each summer with the kids, and of Poochie, the mixed beagle the kids begged him to keep, which he did; but then he would catch himself and chase it all out of his mind, as if with a torch. He found himself wondering, too, what was happening to his money, and he wrote a note to each kid in big black letters: I KNOW HOW MUCH MY PENSION AND SOCIAL SECURITY IS. And when Mark came one Sunday he told him that he wanted a lawyer.

"What do you want a lawyer for?"

"I want a lawyer."

"It'll cost you money."

"Just get me a lawyer!"

A lawyer came, and the captain told him that he wanted an exact accounting of his money. He also suddenly realized that he didn't know which of his kids was paying his bills, and the lawyer reminded him that while he'd been at Rosemarie's house he had given her power of attorney, but that he shouldn't worry.

"What d'you mean don't worry? That bitch'll take all my dough. She'll rob me blind. No more signin' checks!"

"I think you'll be more protected if you let her handle the bills rather than have these people bill you. And I'll see that you get an accounting. I was talking to your daughter and she says that all but thirty-nine dollars of your pension and Social Security is going to the home. And she sends the home fifteen of the thirty-nine dollars every month for you to use as spending money. You know the office has spending money for you, don't you?"

He knew he went to the office for money any time he wanted

something from the soda machine or some candy, but he had never thought about where it came from. He found himself becoming confused, but he didn't want the lawyer to know it, so he said sternly, "O.K., O.K.," and felt even more trapped than ever because he'd forgotten how to handle money.

Out of nowhere, Punchie said, clear as hell, "Captain, what was you captain of?"

He looked at him sullenly. "Detectives."

"You a cop? Hey!" But just then an aide, walking by, said to Punchie angrily, "Why did you take that string? That was bad . . . bad . . . *baad*!"

The captain whirled on her. "Leave 'im alone!"

But she completely ignored him and took Punchie by the arm. "Now you show me that string."

From the time he was a patrolman he always tried to give a guy a break as long as it wasn't a real offense or a guy didn't give him any lip in front of someone. He would take lip sometimes if it was one-to-one, just him and the guy, but not if there was a crowd. Then you couldn't let yourself be showed up, like that broad showing him up in front of all these people. And Talk-Talk, that little bimbo in the chair, was making it worse.

"'Leave him alone?' Ho! You expect her to listen to you? She's one of those who don't listen to you! When I was a surgeon, that baby would be out in the street! They used to stand up when I walked in. Here, I'm cuckoo!"

His immediate impulse was to go for his gun, that fatass son of a bitch broad. But he knew that was crazy, he had to be careful here from now on.

But there was fire in his brain the next couple of days. He tried to relax watching TV one night, but that only threw on gasoline: there was something in the news about a landlord kicking some old people out of an apartment house.

He fantasized going after the bastard, whoever he was, wherever he was, and sticking the rod up against his nose and saying, "What for? What'd you do that for?" and then just blasting away.

But he didn't even know his name. Even if he did, so what?

He leaned back against his chair, thinking of the albino again.

7

The next morning he went to the lounge, but they hadn't set out any of the day's newspapers yet. He had to wait close to an hour. But it was worth it because there on the second page was the story with a picture. The picture showed the bastard standing outside a courtroom, and a couple of old people standing off to one side. The captain read only fragments of the story, just enough to know that the bastard had won some kind of lawsuit evicting these people.

What's more, the captain thought he looked familiar. It took a while, then he remembered. The guy had a neighborhood law office over in the old Fourteenth Ward.

He sat thinking what to do. Then he fished around in his pocket for some change, but he had none. He went into the office and asked if he could have fifty cents of his money. The secretary went to a file and took out an envelope and changed a dollar and gave him fifty cents, which he counted carefully. Going into one of the two phone booths near the lobby, he dialed information, then gave the name, Carl Leonard, and the address that he had copied carefully from the newspaper onto an envelope he'd found. The operator gave him the number, which he had her repeat three times until he marked it down right with the stump of a pencil.

He forgot how much change he would need, and put in too much and started to dial the number, then hung up quickly. In his day you couldn't trace local pay phone calls, but he didn't know how it was today. He went back to the wing. A phone was on the nursing station counter, but a couple of nurses were there. He stood by the door to his room, looking on. One soon rose and walked off, then the other came to the room next to his and spoke to someone from the doorway. He went over to the station, holding the envelope in one hand, and reached over and dialed the number slowly.

"Captain," the nurse at the doorway called to him, "that's a no no."

"Carl J. Leonard," a woman said.

"You open any evenings?"

"Yes, Wednesday and Friday till nine."

He hung up as the nurse approached him. "Captain, you're not supposed to do that. You're supposed to use the pay phones."

"Want talk to my son."

"You reach him?"

He shook his head. She said, "Why don't you go to the office and have someone dial him for you?"

He nodded and, deliberately, shuffled off. He stood outside, wondering what he could say to the albino, how he could work it. As he stood there on the veranda even the houses across the street suddenly seemed so far away, as though that world lay beyond a wall now. It called back a feeling he'd had on several occasions, knowing a killer was across the state line, pretty sure where he was but afraid of risking that line. A county line was one thing, a state line something else. He had never crossed a state line.

Sundays the parking lot was crowded, and Mark had to maneuver around before he found a spot. He sat in the car for a few moments, looking at the home. He always dreaded going in. And the murder didn't help. Though he was sure it had nothing to do with the care—it was the best home they had seen—the murder threw a kind of shadow on it.

Ellen should never have insisted Pop come live with her unless she was going to keep him, he thought. Still, he couldn't really blame her, because her husband would say—and he had every right to—what about my father, he's in a nursing home, what about him? Rosemarie . . . well, she really and truly was selfish, all out for herself. And he himself never felt particularly close to the old man, and he really didn't have room for him. He'd had to double the kids up to give the old man a bed.

But why should a guy forty-two still feel guilty?

The old man had never been *bad* to him, and he had even been proud to have a father who rode a nice shiny motorcycle and had a uniform. Although some of the other kids used to give him that old one about, "What's your father do? Oh, he doesn't do anything he's a cop," he knew they were jealous that he had the motorcycle which he always used to gun as he parked it in front of the house. And when he was made head of vice and his name started being in the papers he used to feel proud of him, too. And, of course, when he was put in charge of the special squad he was the biggest-name cop in the city. The trouble was he was *all* cop. God, he was out almost every night.

"Pop, I think I want to take up accounting or something to do with business."

"Sure. Great."

But he had been concentrating on something else when he answered. Mark felt he might have said, "Pop, I want to be a dancer," and he would have gotten the same response.

In the building now, he looked around the main lounge, went back to his father's room, and eventually found him in one of the smaller lounges. The TV was on but he wasn't looking at it—just sitting there staring ahead.

"Hi, Pop."

The captain looked at him wordlessly.

"Pop, there's big doings at Rosemarie's today. It's Lou's birthday and she's making a family dinner. So . . . why don't you put on your suit?"

"Ain't goin'."

"Pop, please. Pop, everyone wants you."

The captain looked at him again. "Why the hell didn't you call?"

"I was . . . sure you'd want to go," he said, awkwardly.

"Could have called, ain't dead yet."

"Pop, we want you."

He wanted to go, God knows he wanted to go, but he felt that he had to say something else. "Called, I coulda gotten in my suit."

He lumbered back to his room. Mark had signed him out at the front desk by the time he came back. The two of them sat silently as they rode. Occasionally, Mark said something about the trees or flowers or the streets, but the captain didn't answer. Riding here with his son, it was as though he hadn't been out in years.

Rosemarie's house even came as new to him. As he walked in, Rosemarie and Ellen kissed him and Rosemarie's husband, Lou, shook his hand and Stewart, Ellen's husband, shook his hand also and clapped his back and said, "It's good seeing you, Captain." He was always "Captain" to his sons-in-law. And the grandchildren, some of them hanging back, some coming forward quickly, kissed him.

"Hey, you're really looking good," Lou said.

And the others took it up. It was as if he was five years old, he thought. He would believe them if they wouldn't carry it on so long.

The TV was on, and that helped. He really wasn't part of the conversation after a while. As he sat there, though, in this home that came back to him fully, it was as if lava were draining from him. He felt perfectly right being here, but with it there soon came a feeling of uneasiness, then of dread, and finally of horror. Here, with the family all around, with the TV playing, with his grandchildren, it really hit him as wrong, all wrong, that he . . . *he* had caused someone to die. It was as though he thought about it for the first time.

"Pop, something wrong?"

He looked around dazedly. It was Ellen.

He shook his head, feeling panicky. Then he thought: let me stay here and I will make it up. That was it. If somehow he could stay here, didn't have to go back, he could come to grips with himself, would go back to the Lutheran Church again and pray for her soul, would ask Jesus for forgiveness just as he would ask Jesus to forgive *her,* forgive everyone who hurt old people. Suddenly, now, the important thing was to stay. But in order to stay he had to do everything exactly right. He must not do anything to make them think he couldn't handle himself, or say anything that would disturb them, make them think he was a nut-o.

So he sat very stiffly. As it came time for dinner he felt his bladder was going to burst. He had to go so bad, but he was afraid he might have trouble finding the bathroom. Not that he *would* have trouble, but he *might,* and he didn't want to ask. Now, as Rosemarie called out, "Dinner," he stood up, but he did have to go and he started up the stairs.

"Pop, where you going?" Mark said.

"I got to make," he said. Christ, why did he say something so childish? But he hadn't wanted to say "to take a piss," which was the only thing he could think of.

"Let me show you where it is."

And before he could say, "I'll find it," Mark was there, even guiding him up the stairs and opening the bathroom door for him. And afterward he was even out there *waiting* for him.

During dinner, he got through the soup fine, didn't spill a thing, but some lettuce fell off his fork and he tried to get it back with his fingers, because he wanted to be *sure* it would get on. It was as though everyone were around him trying to help. And the kids and grandkids were looking at him strangely. Rosemarie even came over to help cut his roast beef.

"I'm not a baby!" It just burst out of him. He wished he could just stuff the words right back in his mouth.

"Whoever," and she seemed to be singing it, "said you were a baby?"

"Lemme alone."

"Rosemarie, just..." Ellen motioned for her to go back to her chair. But he was so upset now that some of the meat kept sliding away from his fork.

After dinner they watched television again, and things seemed to work out so well that he had hopes again. But then Rosemarie said, "Pop, Lou and me will drive you back," and it was as though thunder filled his head, and someone was helping him on with his jacket now, and there were kisses and handshakes all around and he was in the car again, sitting in the back like some kid-prisoner on his way to the can, saying nothing, staring straight ahead. They were in the parking lot now and Rosemarie said, "Lou, I'll be right back," and she stepped out and opened the captain's door. Lou said, "Captain, you look good, you really do," and the captain was walking with Rosemarie up the steps. But at the door he stopped. And he said the words he didn't want to say.

"Rosie, take me home."

"Oh, Pop."

"Take me home."

"Pop, don't do this to me." Her eyes were wet.

"Do to you?" He stared at her, chest pumping. And then it simply shot out: "What the fuck doing to you?"

"Pop," her face was stern now, "I don't want that language any more!" Then she said, "Do you want us to find you a different place? Maybe you don't like this one. We'll get you a different place."

"You mean cheaper, huh? And put away more of my dough!"

He flung the door open and strode in. She came in also but didn't follow as he pushed open the doors to Wing B.

Get me a machine gun! God, get me a machine gun!

And in the lobby Rosemarie stood watching the closed doors to the wing. It was as if he had read her mind. Not that she . . . would have done it. But it had crossed her mind. A cheaper place, then maybe they could save money for the kids' education.

He went straight back to his room and hit at the venetian blinds, and they flew about with a great clattering. It brought in an aide but he didn't even look at her when she asked what was wrong, was afraid he'd leap for her throat. After a while, hearing her leave, he took off his jacket and kept lashing it at the bed.

But he couldn't release the fury in him.

Slowly, he drew out the crumpled envelope from his pocket, turned on his overhead light and straightened out the envelope to make sure he hadn't smudged the address.

8

The only thing the police knew for sure about the murder was that the bullets were .38s. They didn't even have a single worthwhile fingerprint; the only few clear ones were the dead woman's. And, up until eight days after the murder, they knew of only two possible suspects. One was a former boy friend of her daughter's whom the victim hadn't liked, and who had gone AWOL from his army base two days before the murder and was still missing. The other was a seventeen-year-old girl named Helene Glenn who had worked in the kitchen and been fired three weeks before the murder when Mrs. Latimore and another nurse reported that she appeared to be on drugs. Furthermore, Helene had been on a work-release program from a nearby center for delinquent girls. She ran away the day she was fired.

Then, as the investigation was in its ninth day, Detective Captain Joseph Denny, of Homicide, walked into LaSala's office in the Police Administration Building. He said, "Cummings, the administrator of the home? Just called. Some guys really think fast," and he snapped his fingers. "He said he just remembered a kid who worked there as an orderly for a couple weeks last summer. They canned him because he was supposed to have hit a patient. Cummings says he's not sure, but he has the feeling Latimore was the one who caught him."

"Last summer? That's a whole year to think about getting even."

"Here's the name and address. Don't say I never gave you anything."

LaSala in turn assigned it to the youngest detective on his squad, Cruse. About an hour later Cruse called him from a payphone.

"Lieutenant, this has possibilities. I'm in a drugstore. I was talking to the druggist before going over to the house. The kid goes to college. And he's in for the summer. So that could be the reason for the year. I was wondering if you still want me to talk to him or should I just bring him in?"

"Bring him in. But, you know, nice, if he don't give you trouble. We still don't have a thing."

He wasn't home, Cruse learned; had a summer job at a hospital. And so Cruse brought him in from there, a tall, long-haired blond kid named Frank Lang, a pre-med at Yale. Although he admitted being fired from the home, he claimed not to know anyone named Latimore. LaSala took from a drawer a snapshot he had gotten from her daughter. It showed a thin-faced woman piled high with blond hair.

"Oh, her. Oh, sure I knew her. But, look, I didn't kill her or anyone else."

LaSala said, "How come you didn't know her name?"

"I knew her name then, but I forgot."

Cruse said, "What's this about you hitting a patient?"

"I never hit a patient. I told her I never hit a patient. And she never saw me hit a patient. But she believed it when this patient said I hit him. And the office believed it too. You want to know what happened? This is the honest-to-God truth. She had this old fellow in restraints—you know, in a vest tied in a chair. That was my first exposure to a nursing home. I hated seeing people in restraints, but I know there are some people who have to be, they'll fall down, they'll break a hip. But I swear this old fellow didn't have to be. He didn't like to wear his false teeth and she made him and he threw them at her and she got the O.K. to put him in restraints. I know, I was there. Anyway, the house rule, as I remember, was that a person could only be in restraints two hours at any one time, then had to be out an hour.

But they used to keep them in all day, because the hour they were out you had to watch them. She, in particular, was great at keeping them restrained. Anyway, I let this fellow—tell you the truth, I let others out too—anyway, I let him out and I was watching him and she came in the room and said what's going on here, why wasn't I doing blah, blah, whatever I was supposed to do. I said I was watching him because he was in restraints long enough and she started yelling at me and he began crying. I think he was crying because he thought she was yelling at him. And he said I hit him. Poor guy, he was confused and I'm sure he was scared. So she took it to the office and they fired me. I'm sure she was just glad to get rid of me."

They asked him for his story for July sixth, the night of the murder, and he couldn't remember at first but then did remember. "I spent all night with my girl."

"What time is all night?" LaSala asked.

"I got home from work about five-thirty and I got to her house about a quarter after six. And I was there until eight-thirty in the morning when I went to work. If you don't believe me you ask her, or if you don't believe her ask her parents."

LaSala felt a little jolt at that. He had friends who had been through this with their daughters, and he had been almost through it himself that time when Annemarie called to say she was staying at her boy friend's house, his parents were home, and he almost dove into the phone after her, telling her to get her ass home, which was something he never once had said to her before. But she got it home.

"Tom, check it out," he said to Cruse.

And it checked.

It was almost half-past seven by the time LaSala got home. Home was a row house with an open porch and an air conditioner in their bedroom and a large fan in the window of what once was Annemarie's room until she got married eight years ago. Their first child, Mike, whom they adopted a year before Katherine became pregnant with Annemarie and they were sure they couldn't have children, had been killed crossing the street when he was only eight. Nicholas LaSala still went to his grave every three or four months.

Katherine warmed up dinner for him; she usually waited to eat with him when she could, his hours were so crazy, but tonight she had promised to go to bingo with her great aunt. It was a good marriage. He often remembered that time he first introduced her to Vinnie, his best friend, and Vinnie, who had just seen this movie, took him aside, said, "What's with blonde? She a Viking?" "You never hearda North Italy, you *cetriòlo?*" Only recently she had told him how she used to worry when he was younger, she knew how some women liked cops. That was true. Some could take on a whole precinct. But he had stayed clear.

He was fifty-one, massive, with strong bowlegs and thinning gray hair. He'd had a brief dream of being a prizefighter but lost all but one of his four amateur fights. He worked in a warehouse for a few years after high school, then had passed the test for the force; but because the captain had tapped him before he'd even finished the academy, he'd had to go back to the academy after that one undercover job before returning to the squad. He stayed with the squad fourteen years, then made detective and moved on. He apparently was good at taking tests up to lieutenant, but never made good enough scores after that. He had reached the point now where even the captain at Homicide was younger.

Well . . . next year this time it was goodbye to all of this. He could have taken his pension long ago but had kept holding off. He still had mixed feelings about leaving, but common sense said grab the pension and go into private security or, if he and Katherine found the right place and got the right financing, run a small motel down the shore. He'd had some good times on the force, had made a lot of important collars, yet in all these years, though he had drawn his gun plenty and used the butt plenty, he had shot only one guy, and him only in the hip. He was proud of that. A lot of the boys, they think you got a gun, you got to use it. Maybe he was lucky. But some of it was using your head, for instance not trying to go in alone and grab a guy in the middle of a job unless it was necessary. Chances are he's jumpy then, tense, ready to panic, will go for a gun if he's got one. But if you waited until he was finished, was walking away, had calmed down, sometimes you could just walk up behind him and put your arm around him and he would just roll his eyes. Or if you had to go in you waited until enough of the boys came and the guy saw he had no chance. Things like that.

But another reason he didn't like leaving—seeing the captain really made him face this—was that it was something else telling you you're getting old.

He found the albino walking someone very slowly toward physical therapy. He waited in the hall until the albino came out alone. "Hey," and he motioned him toward a side door. Outside, in the warm sun, he said, "I want a ride Wednesday night."

"Oh, no. No more, Captain."

"I don't want no crap from you, hear?"

"This ain't no crap. I ain't lookin' for trouble."

"You're looking for trouble right now you fucken faggot!"

"What you want to call me names like that for?"

"I'm goin' to the office and telling you suck!"

"Captain, you promised me. You said just that one time."

"Two times now. Just two."

"Hey, whyn't you ask your chilrun?" he said as though he never thought of this before.

"I'll give you ten bucks."

"Captain, I don't want your money. I don't want no trouble. Now whyn't you ask your chilrun?"

This was getting scary; he didn't want him doing too much thinking. If only this was the old days. A quick knee to the balls, this son of a bitch would drive him coast to coast.

He was so close to swinging at him, was so frustrated, so enraged that he made himself walk away. Something crazy like that, they'd tie him up. He was hoping the albino would change his mind and come after him, but when he stopped by the rose bushes and looked back the bastard was gone. Frantic, he tried to think what to do. He pictured himself going to the parking lot at night and finding a key in a car or else jumping one. He'd jumped a lot of cars, but he didn't know about the new ones, if you could still do them the same way. He didn't want to risk getting caught just going out there hoping.

He felt so walled-in thinking of all those cars out there, and how easily people slid into them and closed the doors and started them up and just drove off. Just to be able to drive off!

A few hours later he thought of Yorky. Why hadn't he thought of

Yorky right away? He was back in town and would do anything for him. Yorky had pulled two stickups at nineteen and had parlayed two-to-fifteen all the way up to eighty years because of three escapes. Two times he went over a wall and one time under a wall, and each time he was caught within a few hours. The captain had grabbed him the last time, sitting in a car he had stolen and driven almost twenty miles with a piece of bone sticking out of his ankle. This was the last escape, one of the over-the-wall jobs. On the drive back to the can Yorky told him how he had screwed together several pipes he stole from the machine shop and managed to climb the wall with it, only to have the thing break in half when he tried to lift it up so he could climb down the other side. "So I'm sitting there on the wall and I take a deep breath and jump and I'm even flapping my arms like maybe I'll fly."

"You should have been able to fly. You're a bird brain."

He must have said something Yorky liked because he kept writing to him from the can about what he was doing and even about what books he was reading, and the captain used to visit him now and then. He was thirty-three when he was paroled and the captain got him a job on the docks and then got him into the construction union. They kept in touch, Yorky even painted his house for him on weekends, but then he didn't hear from him for about four years. Then a letter reached him at Rosemarie's a few days before he went for the operation. Yorky said he was back in town, would like to see him again, had learned he was staying at his son's. Actually, the letter had come to him at Mark's and Mark sent it to him. The captain never got back to him.

Two aides were using the pay phones and he didn't want to waste time waiting to call information, so he got one of the phonebooks, held it under the light and turned pages to the Y's. But though he turned and twisted his head, thinking it might be his glasses, he couldn't find any Yorky. He took the book into the office and asked the girl there if she could locate a Yorky for him. But she confirmed there was none.

"You know where he lives? You could write to him?"

He had to wait for a skinny crotch-scratcher who came in. "Charlie Holly wants money for cigarettes," he said, scratching away.

"Charlie Holly already smoked a pack today," she said.

"Charlie Holly wants money for cigarettes."

"All right, Charlie Holly, here's money for one more pack. Now don't forget, this is your money and if you're going to use it all up you won't have any more money." She seemed to have forgotten the captain, for after Charlie Holly left she started to go back to her typewriter. Then she looked up at him with some surprise.

"He just moved into town."

"Who?"

Don't treat him like a fucken crotch-scratcher, you cunt. "Yorky."

"I really don't know what to say," she said.

He walked out. He started back to the wing, then had an idea and went to the phone and dialed information. He asked if there was a new listing for a Yorky. She asked for a first name but though he hit at his head he couldn't remember. "Just try Yorky." There was a listing for a Yorky, John, and he marked it down. But when he called, the girl who answered said Mr. Yorky wasn't in, could he return the call? "Tell him it's Captain Hughes. Call me." And he carefully read off the numbers on the phone.

Sometime that evening he saw Garbo coming for him. "Someone's calling you on the pay phone."

There he picked up the dangling receiver. "Yorky?"

"Hey, Captain, it's real good to hear you. I was worrying what happened."

"I want to see you. Can you come here tomorrow?"

"Sure, where are you?"

"I'm in a nursing home, Yorky. They put me in a fucken home." He felt his lips begin to tremble. He bit at them.

Yorky made a sound that wasn't quite a groan and not quite a sigh. "Which one is it, Captain? Where are you?"

"Hold on." He suddenly couldn't think of the goddamn name. And if there was anything Yorky mustn't think, it was he was nuts. He knew the name—he knew it like his own name. He opened the door as a man waddled by on two canes. "Where are we?"

"And yourself, sir." The prick was waiting for an answer. The captain pulled the door closed . . . Oh, Christ yes. "It's called Linwood. Look up the address."

"I'll see you tomorrow, Captain."

In his room, he took out the envelope with the address on it and tried to figure out where in the Fourteenth Ward it came in. No one could have known this city, its streets and alleys, better than he; he'd always been out there touring, prowling. But the last time was ten, eleven years ago, things changed. And it was even hard thinking through to what it was then. But he was getting certain streets in place now, maneuvering them around until they fit. There were certain gaps, though. He would fill them in eventually if he just wouldn't panic.

9

Yorky was there at nine. But they made him wait for visiting hours, which didn't begin until ten-thirty. The captain, summoned to the front lounge, saw him standing near the tropical fish, tall, broad, almost totally bald now. The captain thought of him as having more hair.

"Hey, Captain, hey there," and he took the captain's hand in both of his. "Hey, you're looking good. This is a hell of a nice place," he said, nodding as he looked around, as if trying to convince someone.

The captain led him to a far corner of the lounge. Yorky drew two chairs together.

"I want you to sign me out tomorrow and take me for a ride." Tomorrow was Wednesday.

"Sure. But I work till three-thirty. Four, four-thirty, all right? But if it's important I'll take off."

"No."

"Any place special you want to go?"

"No. Just a ride. Yorky? Can I stay the night? I want a night outta here."

"Sure." He cleared his throat. "So. Hey, you're looking good."

"Yorky, just hear this. I ain't see-nile. I don't piss myself, I don't crap myself, I can read, I can hear, I can talk."

"You sound great to me. I'm fifty-eight myself, you know."

"Kids. You . . . get to be a pain in the ass to 'em." But he'd better stop. He was afraid he'd sound nuts.

"Hey, you want to go for a ride now?"

"No."

"Why not? What you got to do?"

"No." But he didn't really know why. He didn't have anything to do, but he didn't want to go out. It was as though something kept him tied here, as if—well, as if this was his office and he had to be here and watch over it, and you don't go anywhere unless you prepare in advance for it.

"Hey, I got married, you know. Guess how old she is? Nineteen. I met her in the hills of West Virginia, we were building a tunnel. I taught her to read and write some. That coulda been a mistake," he laughed. "She thinks I'm the greatest. And I think that's the greatest."

The captain felt a twinge of envy, but as Yorky talked on he found it hard not to fall asleep. He was exhausted from tension, from being up part of the night wondering if Yorky would really show up. And it wasn't over yet, he had more to ask of him and more to remember about the streets.

The next day Yorky arrived much earlier than he'd said, at three, but the captain was already in the lounge waiting for him, holding a brown paper bag because someone had lifted his goddamn suitcase. Part of his pajamas showed at the top. He had underwear in there too, at the bottom, but between the underwear and pajamas was the gun. The box of bullets was in his pants pocket, and he had his jacket on.

"Lemme take it, Captain."

"No."

They started to walk out, but the girl at the desk said you had to sign out, so Yorky did. In the car, he threw his yellow hard hat from the front seat to the back. After he started it up he said he was running a bulldozer on this job. He could run just about any piece of heavy equipment, he said, but he loved the big cranes. "Owe that to you, Captain," he said, "all to you."

He was angry that the captain was in a home. Three kids and he had to be in a home! He rarely got angry, but this got him. Most of the time he didn't feel very much one way or the other, just went along with things, the good and the bad. Way back then, even, those two heists weren't his idea. This other guy said let's knock the ol' service station over, then there was the clothing store, and he just went along—had nothing better to do, he didn't want to let the guy down, and he could use the bucks. And two of the times he broke out of the can it was someone else's idea; didn't want to louse them up.

He probably would even have killed a guy in the same way, without anger, just because the guy was in the way of a job or a break. He wasn't sure about that, though. But there were a lot of things he wouldn't do: he would never screw a friend, never hit a woman, never take a beer from a guy without buying next, never curse in front of a lady or kids, never hit a homo without a reason. And he wouldn't pull any more jobs, not that he had any feelings against it, it just was dumb; like the captain had said, "You're being dumb, Yorky."

"Hey, where'd you like to ride to?"

"Around the city. Ain't really seen it for so long." He saw, soon, that Yorky took that to mean along the river and into the parks and through all the nice spots, but as the city came into focus more and he found, to his excitement, that he was able to predict a lot of the streets that came up, he gradually eased Yorky over to the Fourteenth Ward. There it was as if something foggy and formless took shape, became buildings, became streets and signs and shops, and then *the* street for a while until they cut off. By the time they headed to Yorky's apartment he was sure he had it clear and kept picking out other landmarks.

He had dinner with Yorky and Victoria, who didn't even come up to Yorky's shoulders and wasn't much wider than one of his forearms. He had trouble swallowing the food, but he got it down. He didn't want to let on he was nervous, and he was still trying to think how he could put it to Yorky, if Yorky would say OK. Later, he played with their little mutt, hoping he wasn't sweating on the face like he was on his neck and chest and down his arms. While Victoria was in the bathroom, Yorky said, "Captain, I would have you live with us, honest-to-God, but we got only the one bedroom and you'd have to sleep on the couch. One night ain't bad, but—Captain, that sounds like a bunch of crap to you, but it's the truth."

"Yorky, I want to borrow your car." There. Fast.

Only Yorky's eyes showed a touch of surprise; but now even that was gone. The captain was sure he was thinking, when's the last time you drove, you got a license, can you see good enough? "Sure. When?"

"Now."

"Let's go. Let me show it to you."

"I need the toilet."

When Victoria came out, he went in with the bag and put the revolver under his belt, in the back. He had to urinate, but had to stand there until he was able to relax enough.

Victoria was frowning slightly, but Yorky was smiling. "Come in any time you want," Yorky said. "Door'll be unlocked."

She added, "If we're not up, I'll have everything ready for you."

Yorky went downstairs with him. All he did was show him where the headlight knob was and how the hand brake worked, because it could be pretty tricky, and apologized that it had over a hundred-thousand miles on it and was really a bucket. He put the key in the ignition and slid out and waited while the captain got in. "See you, whenever," and he didn't even wait to see if he had trouble starting it. Which he did. The motor kept grinding away, so he finally turned it off and waited a while. This time it caught. It was not quite dark yet, a light gray. He switched on the lights, anyway, but it was the windshield wipers, and he fumbled around until he turned them off and found the right knob.

It was six, seven years since he'd driven at all.

He released the hand brake and gave it a little gas and it moved forward slowly. He gripped the wheel hard.

God, where the hell was he?

Suddenly, he'd forgotten every direction.

He kept driving on as though in a tunnel, the sweat oozing out of him, icy, afraid that somehow the car would leap forward on its own. He kept stepping on the brake to stop and get out, but each time he let up. Then he saw a church ahead, and as he got close he remembered they'd passed it on the way to Yorky's apartment. The street after that you turned right. Or left? No, right.

He turned, and it looked familiar. It *was* familiar, and he knew you went along here until you reached Cambridge Street, which he would know by the ice cream parlor on the corner, and there you definitely turned left. When he made that turn he relaxed a little, but only a little.

Sometimes, Gordie used to drive. Gordie was his sergeant for fourteen years, big, a nice chocolate brown, never flustered—used to give it to his own even more than to whites. "You ever get kicked in the balls, man?" And the guy that time, denying for as long as he could that there was any stuff in the house, was so frightened he nodded, even though he didn't seem to understand. "Well, you gonna get kicked again."

Or when they broke into the house that time, maybe ten of them, not counting reporters, and Gordie—or was it Vince then?—whoever—playing up to the reporters when they woke this guy at night and he lay staring up at all the faces. "If you don't get dressed fast, we ain't gonna take you."

What times!

But mostly he drove, and sometimes, on a big crackdown, there would be cars fanning out all over town, or there would be four, five in a line, the guys sitting shoulder-to-shoulder.

You were always tense on a big one. Like now.

Hey, the street!

He was halfway past when he recognized it and he turned right, though he wasn't sure about that. He would give it twenty blocks before turning back. But by the ninth block he saw it, a corner storefront. He found a spot across the street and parked there, the motor still on, looking over. On the window it said Carl J. Leonard, Attorney at Law, and to one side, and lower, Real Estate.

The captain remembered him well because Leonard was a city councilman for two terms, but didn't run again when one of the newspapers linked him with a sleazy collection agency. There was a trial, but after he was cleared—even before he was cleared—there was talk about his paying off his honor the fucken Judge Blasswell, who had foot-long pockets under his robes. But it just stayed talk.

He was a young man then, Leonard, maybe thirty at most and, from some who knew him, a millionaire a few times over. Though he worked out of this little office, he had, at least back then, a castle in the suburbs.

Kicking out old people!

Though he was aflame with anger, and took the gun out of his belt and put it in his pocket, he thought of another way he might handle this. Maybe he could just go up to Leonard, who would surely remember him, and say something like, "Give these people a break. It's shitty being old." Christ, how many times he had smoothed things out for people. He could almost hear the voices. "Cap'n, that guy won't give me my money back." "Betsi threw my clothes out. I messed around only once. Only once in my life." "Talk to Frankie, Captain. I'm scared for my boy, those boys are bums." He never failed to go, and usually he was able to patch things up.

He got out of the car; he would simply talk to him.

Crossing the street, he didn't mind when he saw a woman through the window, Leonard's secretary, sitting right outside the back office. He opened the door. A bell sounded, and she looked up from a book. "Can I help you?"

"Mr. Leonard."

"Do you have an appointment?"

He shook his head. She went to the open door of the office, said something there, then turned to him. "You can go in."

Leonard stood up from his desk, jowly, his belly out to here. The captain started to say something, but it was as though his brain had burst, words wouldn't come, he was half blind with fury, and he reached in his pocket and got the gun and held it out toward where the fucker's heart should be and squeezed the trigger. There was a great gush of red and he fired again, then ran out and the woman was standing in his way, and he fired right into her open mouth. He ran out the door and across the street. His hand was shaking, but the key found the ignition and the motor roared, and he made a sharp right against a red light, then a left down the first street, then a few more, and finally he slowed up and just kept driving, totally lost in the night.

He pulled up to a curb and dropped his head against his arms folded across the wheel. His head was throbbing, everything was throbbing, but he couldn't stay, he had to get away from here. He drove on, going deeper into nowhere.

He turned into street after street, driving a few blocks, then turning again.

Less than half in the tank.

It was three in the morning when the unknown street he was on opened to Webster Avenue, a main drag he recognized. And he knew, whether it was to the right or left, that Yorky's street cut into it. It turned out to be left.

As they'd promised, the door to the apartment was open, and a small night light was on.

10

The Homicide Division was made up of three squads, two of which worked on current murders, while the third worked on cases that were unsolved after about a year. Each was headed by a lieutenant who reported to Detective Captain Denny, who in turn reported to Detective Inspector McDowell, the first black commander of the Division.

Two shopkeepers called the police simultaneously, and the alarm went out in several directions—to Homicide, to the Fourth Precinct, and to all squad cars in the city, five of which raced to the scene. One of Detective Lieutenant Welsh's men got the call in Homicide. Since it was a big one, a double, before leaving with one of the boys he contacted Welsh at his home. Welsh drove there, too, as did Captain Denny, who also had been notified.

Welsh and Denny got there within a minute of each other, just before nine. One police floodlight was on, but they were having trouble with the other. Two television crews were there, and behind the ropes were growing hordes of people.

Carl Leonard, who had been pronounced dead at the scene, was still lying in back of his desk. The chair that had tumbled on him had been moved to one side. His wife, who had been substituting for his secretary, had been rushed to the hospital unconscious. A detective had gone with her.

While the lab men were at work, this much was known in addition to the victims' identities: Leonard had two hundred and thirty-eight dollars and change in his pocket, his wife had a little over twelve dollars in her purse, and there were no signs of ransacking, which meant it was either something beside robbery or the killer had panicked. And the killer was a man, probably alone.

A number of shopkeepers, their customers, and residents had heard the shots. All but three of them, however, had thought it was a car backfiring, firecrackers left over from the Fourth, or their imaginations. Of the three who immediately knew they were shots, one had been on the toilet and another, after convincing his wife they were shots, couldn't get past her as she screamed and pushed at him not to go out. The third had rushed out and seen a man run across the street, get into a car on the driver's side, and race off.

"I'm not sure, but I think he was a colored guy," he told Welsh, repeating his story. "I didn't get all that good a look at his face, but he looked colored. And he had on a jacket o' some kind."

"And the car?"

"The make? Like I told you guys, I don't know, I ain't good at that. But it was a two-door, and no new job. I tried to get the license but, Christ, he went around the corner like crazy. Like I said, it was either dark green or black."

Word soon came over the police radio that one of the squad car boys just spoke to a man about ten blocks from here who'd seen a car speed by. Welsh passed it on to Captain Denny.

"Ready for this one?" he said, glumly. "A new Chevy, yellow. He couldn't see the driver, but there was a woman passenger."

"*Great.* We're in good shape."

The next news was worse. Mrs. Leonard had died without regaining consciousness.

Carl Leonard, they learned almost immediately, was the former councilman who had been in the news off and on for the past eight months or so. He had purchased a small, fairly run-down apartment house about two years ago and this year sent eviction notices to the tenants, most of them elderly, claiming they had broken their leases. Their argument was that they had gotten together and refused to pay rent until Leonard restored the services he had cut drastically. A citizens' group, the Alliance for Human Beings, formed quickly and began picketing the building and raising funds to fight the case. Not only had they lost, they didn't know if they could raise enough money to appeal.

So, the motive could lie somewhere in this, or in their personal lives, or in some business deal. And you still couldn't rule out robbery.

The captain opened his eyes, closed them again to get more sleep, then remembered with a start where he was, what happened. He sat up fast. Yorky and Victoria were having breakfast in the nook off the living room; both smiled at him.

"We wake you?" Yorky asked. "We tried to keep it down."

He shook his head, his eyes going to his jacket which he'd dropped to the floor along with everything but his underwear and socks. He wondered had the gun slipped out, where it was under that pile.

"Look, we ain't gonna look, you get dressed," Yorky said. "Or you can keep sleeping. Sleepy?"

He shook his head again, and when they turned he felt through his clothing until he made sure the gun was in the jacket pocket, then he gathered it all up and took it into the bathroom. He put on his pants first, stuck the gun in the belt.

"Ain't you hot?" Yorky said when he came out wearing the jacket.

"No."

"You being formal? We ain't formal. . . . Wear what you want, feel at home. What'll you have, Captain?"

"Little coffee."

"How about juice, eggs, toast?"

"Coffee's O.K." They didn't have the morning paper. He was glad they didn't have the paper.

He had trouble drinking the coffee, though, because his right hand began to shake when he picked up the spoon. It wasn't just nerves; he felt drained and everything hurt, his shoulders, arms, back, legs. He picked up the cup and some coffee sloshed over.

Yorky and Victoria pretended not to notice.

He tried the left hand and, for some reason, that was better. But he didn't finish. He wiped his lips on a paper napkin.

Yorky said, "You want to stay the day? Whyn't you stay, I'll be back after work. You and Vickie, you can take a walk."

"No. I gotta go back." He was worried something had gone wrong, they might be waiting for him there. He would rather know than not know.

"Sure thing."

Victoria held out her hand at the door and he shook it. Yorky didn't say much as they drove. The captain was glad, didn't want to hear a voice, for he was growing more nervous as they came close; he was starting to feel nauseated.

Parked outside the home, Yorky said he'd be keeping in touch and they would do this plenty. After the car pulled away, the captain couldn't remember if he'd said goodbye or thanks; he had wanted to. Looking at the front door, he felt the urge to turn, to run. His legs almost didn't make it up the steps. They were good strong legs, but today they were rubbery. He opened the door and the girl behind the desk looked up with a smile, and a guy with a piss bag attached to his wheelchair was being pushed past the lobby. He let out a little sigh.

He saw a newspaper on one of the chairs, and the tension came back as he picked it up. There it was on the front page. He read only the first couple paragraphs, then put the paper down and went to his room. He had been troubled about the woman, though as his secretary she had been that bastard's accomplice. An accomplice was just as guilty as the triggerman. Now, her being his wife made them completely one.

"Captain, did you have a nice outing?" It was Garbo. He realized only now that she hadn't been working mornings for a while.

"Yeah. Good."

And he meant it.

He felt strong and as clearheaded as if he had taken in lungsful of good ocean air. It was a long time since he felt he had a purpose.

Three days later LaSala got a call from the assistant superintendent of Streamview Acres, the center for delinquent girls, who told him that Helene Glenn had been picked up and returned there. He added, with some embarrassment, that she had actually been returned four days ago but there had been a slipup, each of them thinking someone else had called the police.

LaSala almost threw the phone across the room. Instead, he walked out of his office and tapped Detective Goldner at his desk to come with him.

Helene Glenn was a fat redhead with a lot of pimples. She didn't know anything about Mrs. Latimore being killed, she said. No, she didn't like her, why should she like her, she got her fired, but she didn't kill her.

"She said I was on dope. I stabbed my stepfather, I completely admit that, and I made it with five guys for my boy friend, and I've boosted from stores, but except for three times I smoked I never took dope in my life. I was taking pills for my menstrual period and I may have looked funny, but I get terrible pains. And then she and that other broad they said dope and I get fired and now I gotta spend all this time. Shit.

"I can tell you things about that place. You know, there's a broad in that kitchen, I ain't mentioning names, she shows her tits to the old guys for fifty cents. There was a guy worked there he used to get this old lady to—you know, blow 'im. Office wouldn't believe her and then someone saw evidence on 'er—it gets me sick to the stomach I think of it. All they did was let him go. Hushed it up. I know one of the old guys there, a whacky, raped three of the old ladies, those poor old ladies, and all they did was send him back to the VA hospital. Hushed it up. Shit."

She said she was at an uncle's farm, a boy friend of her uncle's really, ever since she was fired to the day she was picked up, and that was one hundred and fifty miles from here, and she never left there once. You could ask her uncle's boy friend. Just call the police there: they had him for harboring a fugitive and, shit, she was seventeen, for corrupting the morals of a minor.

LaSala and Goldner left her, feeling as if their brains were spinning in their skulls. They made the call from Homicide and the local police said they would question the boy about it. And, as LaSala and Goldner rather expected, the police called back to say her story held up.

This left them with only one possible suspect, Latimore's daughter's former boy friend who went AWOL. LaSala knew he had better check on this to make sure he, too, hadn't been picked up in the meantime. He hadn't.

Although LaSala wasn't actively involved in the Leonard investigation, the reports came to him and he was aware, but not particularly excited about it, that the two bullets they'd been able to check—the third was too smashed—were .38s, and that Ballistics was running comparison tests with the Latimore bullets. But there were lots of .38s out there in the wrong hands. In fact, two of the four other unsolved murders his squad was working on involved .38s.

Toward the end of the week Inspector McDowell called him on the intercom. The words snapped out. The Latimore and Leonard bullets matched. The gun was a .38, probably either a Smith & Wesson or a Ruger.

"Keep this clamped until you hear from me. That's from the boss. I'm meeting with him in a few minutes."

11

Shortly after he returned from his meeting with the commissioner of police, Inspector McDowell called in Captain Denny, Lieutenants LaSala and Welsh, and Sergeant Christy from LaSala's squad. The word he brought from the commissioner was a warning they were to pass on to their men, that anyone who made any comment on the murders to reporters faced immediate suspension and a hearing for dismissal. All statements were to come from, or be cleared by, him or the information officer. Although this was a longstanding rule, it was one that a lot of officers bypassed, becoming "an informed source in the department" to their favorites in the media. Though this probably still wouldn't stop some of them, the commissioner wanted the consequences hammered home again, because this was one of those cases that had the potential of triggering widespread fear. It was important not to seed it further with speculation and the tips and rumors that were bound to flood them once the link between the crimes hit the news.

"Now, it's very easy for us to jump to a wrong conclusion in this case," Inspector McDowell said. "The only apparent connection between the murders, of course, is that the nurse and Leonard were involved with old people. But we've got to keep our minds open to other possibilities. One is that Mrs. Latimore was killed for some personal reason, and the killer then hit the Leonards to throw us off, to make us *think* it has something to do with old people."

LaSala waited for him to go on because he'd said "possibilities" and that was only one. The inspector was looking around the conference table now, a guy LaSala had really learned to respect, though once he gave himself a laugh wondering if he ever pulled off the necktie at home and yelled muddah fuck, because he not only talked what one of the boys called "perfect north," he was the only cop LaSala never heard curse. LaSala said, "One of the things that gets me is, all right someone had something against Leonard, he was kicking out old people—and the wife, she was killed, she was in the way—but the nurse? She was *helping* them. You go out there, you hear only good."

"I'd suggest going back over her records, talking to the families again," Welsh said.

No shit, you shit, LaSala thought, burning him with his eyes. Nothing better Welsh would like than him falling on his ass with his balls under him. Although they would all stay involved, he and his squad were the principal Homicides on it now, since they had the first murder.

"It could be," Captain Denny said, "a new kind of terrorist gang or a guy with a thing for the old who never even knew the nurse, just wanted to kill someone from a nursing home."

"If so, he picked the wrong place," LaSala said. "There are plenty of real holes around. That's a nice place, far as these places go."

"A nut's a nut. Anyway, let's go over what we got. We'll be trying to trace gun registrations, but you know the chance we got there. It's tough enough even when you're sure of the make. We're checking out the people in the Alliance, we're after the guy AWOL. And, Sam," he said to Welsh, "those names."

Welsh had gotten from Leonard's appointment book the names of three men who were supposed to see him that night. One had been in at seven about buying a building, and his story held up. But the police hadn't yet been able to locate the other two—a J. Clements, no address listed, who had an appointment at eight, and a T. Cohen, also no address, who was scheduled for ten to nine, almost exactly the time of the killings.

Welsh passed the names to LaSala. He studied the paper, then said, "The guy at seven you saw, can I see a report on him? Might want to doublecheck."

Sure, Welsh said. This time his eyes were doing the burning.

The day's first newspaper headline on the latest development was the kind the police were worried about.

TERROR KILLER
AVENGING AGED?

LaSala, reading it at his desk, flung it to one side. It was the sort of thing that not only could further whip up the juices of the killer, but could set off a fuse in the dark brain cells of every crazy in the city.

Yet, you couldn't blame the papers, they weren't making it up. This was a frightening thing, could become a real bloodbath.

He was about to leave to question some of the Leonards' relatives and friends when a call came that had him standing at his desk, motioning to a detective out there to put on a trace.

"I'm not going to give you my name, I don't want to get involved," a man's voice said. "But there's something you ought to look into. That nursing home kicks people out. They take your money and then they kick you out. They took over sixty thousand dollars from us in five years, but when we said we didn't have any more, could they keep Mom as a Medicaid case, they said no and kicked her out. They said for us to come get her, otherwise they'd just ship her home, but we figured they wouldn't do that—after all, over sixty *grand*. But they did. They took her to my sister's house, she wasn't even there, only her daughter, a little kid, the kid didn't even know what was what. They just rang the bell and she answered and they walked Mom just inside the door and left. If they did that to us they do it to a lot of people."

The line went dead, too soon for a trace.

LaSala drove to the home. The administrator was on the phone a while but then came out and took him into his office. Cummings didn't seem fazed by the story. LaSala had had the feeling he would be embarrassed enough to deny it or to change it drastically.

"Yes, we've had to do that on occasion. People are funny. They can't or won't take care of their parents and they put them in here—or *any* home—and they not only dump them, they try to dump their guilts on us. We explain to them very carefully before they sign up, this is a private pay facility. We don't take Medicaid cases. We can't afford to give the kind of skilled care we give on what Medicaid would pay us. Now we explain this to them. We tell them, if you can't afford it find a home that *does* take Medicaid patients. Oh, but they don't want that! They want their parents to have the best. So we say to them, look, your money's going to last two years, four years, ten years, whatever. And they say fine, Pop's not going to live that long. But Pop *does* live that long. And they get mad at us when we say we can't keep him."

LaSala said, "This one where a kid answered the door, does that sound familiar? Can you give us a name?"

"I don't remember anyone mentioning a *kid*," he said thoughtfully. "But I'll check. We usually send a couple orderlies."

"But you can give me the names of everyone you've sent home, can't you?"

"Within the past year, yes. There were only two. And I probably can come up with some over the years."

"I'm also thinking of people you may not have *sent* home, but the family agreed to pick up."

"Lieutenant, now you're really asking a lot. That happens frequently."

"Well, any that really stick out, where there was a quarrel or out-and-out hard feelings."

"But that wouldn't have anything to do with Mrs. Latimore. She wasn't involved in the financial arrangements."

"Did you see today's paper?"

"Yes, someone showed me. And that has me very disturbed. Now people will think she *must* have done something to a patient. It's a tragedy about these two people, I feel sorry for them, but Kay was a fine, capable nurse. There's no connection at all."

"That's why it might be someone who has a grudge against the home itself."

Cummings thought. "Oh, this is great, just great. It's funny how I didn't let myself think about it that way. I saw the story, I thought poor Kay, it's even worse for you now. You're right, though. People are going to think if it wasn't her who was the villain it has to be the home. You know something? You know how many reporters were here? Every story that came out, it was just that she worked in a nursing home and had a fine reputation. But not one word about the home itself, that it's a beautiful place, that we give the best care. The only nursing homes they write about are the rat traps . . . I'll do what I can for you, Lieutenant. But if it's some son of a bitch who has some crazy gripe about this place, I'm going to demand the papers take pictures here and publish 'em!"

LaSala went to a nearby office where two of his men were going over the charts of Kay Latimore's patients, reading her notes. Before the murder of the Leonards they had gone through four months' notes but had found nothing exceptional—medications, side effects, "expired as of . . .," recommendations for restraints or transfers, abusive language from patients, incontinence, incontinence, incontinence. Still, they had questioned a number of families who *might* have been angry at her, without coming up with even a hint of a suspect. Now they were going back over the notes, studying certain incidents much more closely.

"This," said Goldner, "is one hell of a job."

LaSala looked at some of the things they'd jotted down for follow-up. Nothing leaped up at him as particularly promising. But some son or daughter or husband or grandchild—Christ, or nephew—might have been so loaded with guilt they blamed Mrs. Latimore for Mama's death, or the need to put Papa in a diaper.

He was going to leave without seeing the captain, he really wasn't up to seeing the poor guy. It still shook him, but he got caught up in some guilt himself and looked around for him. When he didn't see him, he asked an aide for his room. As he stood in the doorway he suddenly felt rather relieved, for the captain was standing looking out his window, and there was a certain look of strength about him. But when LaSala said, "Captain," and the captain turned, he saw he was wrong: it was as though, in the effort of turning, he had released a valve in himself and all the fluids went out and the bones went soft.

"How've you been, Captain?" He was standing next to him. "I'm LaSala. Nick LaSala."

The captain kept looking at him. Then, "La-Sal?"

"That's right! Anything I can do for you, Captain?"

He shook his head slowly.

"Well . . . got to beat it." LaSala held out his hand. It was several moments before the captain raised his. It felt so feeble.

Sometimes David would buy a newspaper on his way home if he had to stop for a red light where they peddled them between cars. But tonight he made the light.

Laura drew up to their drive at just about the same time he did. He got out of his car and waited for her to pull in. She gave him her cheek to kiss. She'd had a *very* good day, her busiest in the shop in weeks, she announced. Anything new? No, everything the same, and he unlocked the front door and gathered up the pile of mail under the slot. He riffled through it quickly, handing her a letter from Karen while he went through the rest, most of which was junk. She read it standing in the living room. "She seems fine," she said, returning it to him. She scratched at her shortish gray hair—she had finally let it go natural—and said, "I'm going to shower," and he nodded, reading the few scrawled lines that apologized for the few lines and thanked them for the African carving they'd thought she would like and ended with "Bob says to say hello." Bob was the boy friend she was living with; they both worked for public relations firms.

That had been tougher for him than for Laura to get used to. In fact when Karen and Jeff—who was backpacking through Europe before returning to law school—had gone off to college, he had been the one who seemed to have the empty nest syndrome. He had analyzed it, was sure it not only meant getting older, but that gone were the ones for whom he'd changed the direction of his career.

Later David went out and brought back a pizza and soda for her and a flounder platter for himself—he ate mostly fish and fowl since his coronary—and afterward, while she talked on the phone, he went into the den to look through some mail he hadn't opened yet. One was a brochure from the Hayward Medical Center, describing some lectures and seminars on geriatrics. He had already attended a few similar ones—"Pharmacologic Treatment of the Aged," "Geropsychiatry: An Overview," and "Cerebral Atrophy." The only ones he might be interested in now were "Hypertension and the Aged," and

"Neurodiagnostic Methodology for the Aged." He'd see. He put it aside, flipped through some medical journals and pharmaceutical firm materials, tossing most aside.

He thought about a paper he was considering writing on transient ischemic attacks in the elderly. That Lyke Pharmaceuticals was reprinting him was still giving him more of a lift than maybe it should, though he had to admit he liked the feeling. And it had started him thinking of other possible subjects. He had a few interesting cases of transient ischemia, and perhaps a paper on the differential might be worthwhile, though he really had nothing new to offer. But that didn't stop other doctors, did it?

He looked through some of his texts on ischemia, made some notes. He looked for about an hour, which was all he felt like giving it right now. When he came out she was still on the phone. From the little he heard he couldn't tell which of their friends was calling with marital problems—they all seemed to be having them. And they all came to her for advice.

The way she would speak it was as though the two of them never as much as quarreled. Oh boy.

Right now they were on one of their long, typical truces, which they could maintain forever if they talked mostly about inconsequential things, such as golf or tennis scores, who they met that day.

He couldn't even remember the last time they'd really kissed. Sex now and then—just now and then, but all right; but when really kissed? Nor did he know whose fault it was, his, hers, both. Yet that was one of the things you didn't talk about; it led only to a quarrel.

She got off the phone about nine, and they both read in the living room, she lying on the sofa. She went to bed about ten-thirty and he continued reading until it was time to turn on the eleven o'clock news.

"Good evening. Here's what's happening . . ."

Soon David was sitting forward in his chair, hearing for the first time that the murders were connected.

"The police say they have found no personal link between Mr. and Mrs. Leonard and Mrs. Latimore. But they refuse to say—publicly, at least—that they've narrowed the motive down to the victims' involvement with the aged."

The face of the commissioner of police flashed on, along with a side view of a young woman interviewer. He was saying, "We're not ruling out any possibility. The move could be almost anything at all. That's all I really have to say at this time . . . Miss Henley, I'm sorry, I'm not going to speculate like that." The commentator came back on. "But is there a killer or killers at large who are out to avenge so-called wrongs against the aged? That fear is very much on the minds of a number of people we have spoken to. None of them, however, would speak to us on camera." But a voice identified as that of a visiting nurse said, "Many of my patients are elderly, and I must say that even though I'm giving them the best care I possibly can I'm still a little concerned. . . ."

The news switched to a threatened strike. David turned the set off, sat staring at the dark screen.

He couldn't say this enough: Kay Latimore had been a hell of a good nurse. She could be tough, she had her quirks like everyone else—but good. And if someone like her could be murdered as a result of her work with the aged, who the hell in this field was safe?

He stopped off at the home the next morning on some pretense; he wanted to see what the feeling was. The only one he spoke to about the murders was Cummings. That was enough. Though Cummings was smiling when he said he ought to get himself a bodyguard, he was obviously worried.

12

The captain woke sometime during the night, sure that if he opened his eyes he would see his older brother sleeping in the bed next to him, and that his sister's room was across the hall and his mother and father's room down the hall next to the bathroom. Something seemed wrong about that, though he wasn't sure what. And even when he became fully aware of where he was, it still took a while for him to place the room properly in his mind, to realize that the door to the hall was to the left of his bed and not in front as it was when he was a kid.

He found himself growing panicky until he put it all in place. Even then, he didn't completely calm down.

Not that he never had this before. He occasionally experienced it after he first got married, but it had been easy then to realize that he must have been dreaming about home and was still enmeshed in it. And even when it sometimes happened in his kids' homes, he was able to relax quickly because, after all, he was with his *kids*.

He felt alone, isolated.

He thought of his father, a big blond guy with a square face, so rugged in his fireman's uniform. Whenever he thought of his father, it was almost always in his uniform. Maybe because he had been laid out in it, his big hands crossed on his chest. He had died fighting a fire; there had not been a burn on him; he had simply dropped dead pulling a hose, a man not quite fifty-one. The captain remembered his aunt saying, "He died a good person's death. He did not suffer, Marie," while others nodded. But this was something he hadn't understood.

The fire had been arson. And they never found the guy.

He couldn't really remember over the years, but he had the feeling that this had a lot to do with his wanting to be a cop.

He lay there listening to Elephant Ears snoring. It was more like the sound he remembered as a kid, blowing a toy pipe under water. His father-in-law, who lived with them until the day he died at eighty-one, used to make sounds like that. He could be a pain in the ass now and then, the old man, but you just didn't kick out old people then. His mother had lived with his sister until she died at seventy-three.

You just didn't kick out old people then.

He was starting to feel better now, thinking of how he had made those two pay.

He fell back to sleep. When he woke again it was morning and someone was yelling in the hall. He knew it was Talk-Talk.

"I got feelings! I am a human being like everyone else! I am no longer an active surgeon, but I am still an active human being! My heart is beating, and that means I am an active human being!"

Talk-Talk could go days without saying a word, and then suddenly would never stop.

"I am very blue! I am de-*pressed*! Don't anybody care?"

The captain got dressed, went to the toilet and then stepped into the hall to go to breakfast. Talk-Talk, who looked like a parakeet wearing glasses, was strapped as usual in a wheelchair stationed against one of the walls. The captain had thought Garbo was on duty; she usually kept him quiet. But it was that skinny part-timer, Reds.

"I need help! I want answers! Don't any of you answer questions?" But Reds was continuing whatever she was doing at the station, head turned from him. Aides continued walking with patients or carrying trays or equipment. One simply patted him on the head as she went by. "You at the station, will you at least give me the courtesy of a look?

I am very blue! Where is that other lady? Where is that pretty nurse? At least she ack-nowledges you're a human being!"

The captain went for breakfast, then sat on the veranda awhile. When he came back in the building several of the residents, some in wheelchairs, were lined up outside the office. Talk-Talk was still at it when he walked back to the wing. "I have pain in my belly! Why don't you believe me I have pain in my belly! The med-i-cation is not working extremely well! Yo! Will you look at me? I am going crazy! I need help! I have always been a courteous man! I had never wanted to hurt anyone in my life! But I am glad about something! I am glad they bumped her off!"

At this, Reds did look up.

"Oh ho, you think I don't know she was bumped off! They talk in front of me like I don't exist! Like I don't have a brain! Let me tell you something. I know that Washington, D.C. is the capital of this country. I know that Canada is north and Mexico is south. I know that there is a Pacific Ocean and an Atlantic Ocean. I even know there is a Red Sea. I know that Sunday comes after Saturday. I know that heartburn is spelled with an 'h.' I've read *The New York Times* for over fifty years. They don't even know what the hell *The New York Times* is. Yet they talk to each other right in front of me like I'm not here. And now I'm not supposed to know she was bumped off! You know something else? If anyone deserved bumping off, she did!"

"Dr. Persky, that's not very nice. That's terrible."

"Oh you talk, do you? Will you answer me some questions then? Why does my belly hurt?"

"You've already received medication for it. There's nothing more to do. Let it work."

"But it still hurts! Hey!" For she was bending over her work again. "Hey! Will you listen to me? Will *someone* listen to me? You're as bad as she was. Don't let me sit here like a mummy! I am a human being! Can I at least have a cigar? You know where my cigars are, can I have a cigar? Hey? I'm going to holler like hell soon! I feel hopeless! I feel helpless! I am going to call the FBI! Where is my son? He sent me cigars! Can I at least have a cigar? Ho! Yo!"

The captain stood there looking on. Talk-Talk turned to him, to other patients, to Reds again. "I have always been a God-fearing person. I would never dream that I would wish someone to get bumped off. They should all get bumped off! A cigar! Is it too much to ask for a cigar?"

The captain walked over to the station. "Hey." She looked up. "Get him a cigar."

"Aren't we all in a good mood?"

But she did get up and get a cigar from somewhere under the counter and unwrapped it as she walked around. Then she handed it to Talk-Talk, who bent over puffing away as she held a lighted match to the tip.

The captain watched for a few moments. Soon he began to walk down the hall again. He glanced into each room. He walked into the other wings, again glancing into rooms, at the people lying in their beds, on chairs, those walking about. He had the feeling he used to get, riding with his boys through the city, stopping into a dive here and there, just checking, observing; the feeling of keeping the innocent safe, the guilty terrified.

That afternoon David got a call at the clinic from Detective Goldner. "Doctor, I hate bothering you again, but as you know we're going over Mrs. Latimore's notes again. And there are references to some more patients Mr. Cummings tells us are yours. Epstein, Mary. Colby, John. VanEllen, Sally. Utera, Anthony. They are yours, aren't they?"

"All but Mrs. VanEllen. She isn't there any longer." They used to call her Sally V., he recalled.

"What we'd like to know from you is if their families had any fits about anything. Now according to the notes, Mrs. Epstein told her family she wasn't getting anything to eat. John Colby fell, no broken bones. Sally VanEllen was, I'm quoting, 'sexually acting out,' and Mrs. Latimore recommended restraints and also 'referral.' Anthony Utera became abusive, and she also recommended restraints for him. Do you recall any of the families becoming upset over any of this?"

"I'm not trying to put you off, believe me, but the office would know if they did. Complaints generally go to the office, rarely to me."

"We've already done that, doctor, but we're double and even triple checking everything we can."

"I understand. O.K. Now I myself never heard a complaint from any of those families. Mrs. Epstein actually puts away quite a meal, but she had complained to her family. I imagine it's a way of getting attention, and I've spoken to them about it and they fully understand. Now, Mr. Colby—it's a miracle he didn't break a hip. Mrs. VanEllen, well, Mrs. Latimore felt she would be better off in a psychiatric facility. The family never put up a fuss that I know about. In fact, I remember speaking to her son and he said to do whatever was best. Now Mr. Utera is still in restraints, but again I never heard a thing from the family. It's for his protection. He definitely will break his hip, his neck."

"Listen, thanks. And sorry to bother. But I'm afraid I'll probably have to be bothering you again."

"That's perfectly all right."

He returned to his work, then stopped briefly, thinking. He recalled that when Kay had recommended putting Sally V. in restraints and shipping her off, he had thought that the poor old gal hadn't done anything more than a lot of patients did, that Kay obviously didn't like her. He hadn't argued with her, though. Since the nurses were the ones who were with the patients all the time, you had to know when it was worth going head to head with them. And the office would prefer losing a patient than a good nurse.

He saw the open handbag on the chair behind one of the nursing stations, the glint of a cluster of keys. He sidled up to a nearby bulletin board, glanced at it, then darted quick looks in every direction. None of the staff was there. Moments later he was walking away, his hand in his pocket, clutching the keys so they wouldn't make noise.

Outside, he put them under one of the small whitewashed rocks that lined one side of the parking lot.

When the three-to-eleven shift left that night he stood by a window as the employees drifted off to their cars. Suddenly one of the nurses got out of hers, began gesticulating to someone in the next car. That guy, an orderly, climbed out, began searching the ground with her. The captain left the window as he saw them enter the building, apparently to look around.

Eventually she made a call to someone to bring her another set of keys.

The car was green, though he wasn't sure of the make. But he would remember it by the bumper sticker. From what he had seen of it, it said LOVE A NUR.

13

Ever since Kay was murdered, Pat would feel gloomy as she drove up to the nursing home, the heavy awareness of a presence tragically gone, which would usually disappear only when she plunged into her work. Now that her death had been tied in with the other two murders, now that it was unlikely to have anything to do with Kay's personal life or was a random killing, she couldn't help feeling an additional sense of fear, as though someone were watching all of them. Today, with the slanting rain hitting the windshield, that feeling of apprehension was even greater.

But it was one of those days that were so hectic that from the moment she walked in she had no time to think of herself. She even had to ask for additional help from the other wings.

The first thing that happened was an aide's announcement that she had just found Mr. Buckley dead. It was no surprise. He had been in a coma and his family had been notified yesterday that it was probably only a matter of hours, and they had been there until after midnight. Pat went into the room with the aide and pushed aside the closed curtain. He was lying on his back, as though staring at one shoulder, eyes half closed. She could tell with a touch he was gone all right, but still she listened with her stethoscope. Then she went back to the station, took out his chart to see which number was listed to call, then she dialed it and swung her chair around so that she wasn't facing the hall. Some calls were extremely hard to make; some, you had either the office or another nurse call for you. But this death in particular came as a blessing.

"Hello, Mr. Buckley." She recognized the son's voice from his hello. "This is Pat Andreoli at the home."

"He's gone," he said instantly.

"Yes. Just a short while ago."

"I was just coming over. Miss Andreoli . . . tell me. Was he in any pain?"

"No. He died very peacefully." She would have said that, anyway, but when she came on she had spoken to Melanie, the night nurse going off, who had said there was no change, that he seemed comfortable. She had been just about to check on him when the aide reported it. She asked the son if the family wished to see him. Many families did.

"No. I'll call the funeral home. Please give away his clothes. There's nothing we want. And I want to thank you, and I want you to thank all the nurses and everyone else for all you people did for Dad."

"Thank you. I'll be sure to tell them. He was a wonderful man and we all loved him."

"Thank you. Thank you so much. I just wished you'd known him when he was himself."

Her next call was to his doctor, Dr. Kliegman, to come in and sign the death certificate. She got his answering service, as she expected, and left the message. Then she summoned a couple of orderlies and accompanied them into the room, and soon she was watching them push the entire bed toward the Cold Room, the body covered by a sheet, and plastic bags filled with the dead man's effects piled around. She loathed this lack of dignity, often demanded a plain litter and protested having to pile on the clothes, but the office, those asses, felt that this concealed a death from most of the residents.

Soon she seemed to be needed everywhere at once. A woman ripped off her colostomy bag at the same time a patient had to have his tracheostomy tube suctioned, two new patients were admitted, a driver from the funeral parlor wanted to know which of the three bodies in the Cold Room was his, Dr. Persky wanted attention, she tried to help Martha coax the captain into recreational therapy, a diabetic showed signs of ketosis and had to be returned to the hospital. Then Terry, an aide, hurried up to her and said, "Mrs. Rainey's gone sour."

She went into Anna Rainey's room, where another aide was waiting, and drew the curtain. She could see the drastic change at a glance. Anna was lying with her eyes wide open, never moving, face to the side, which caused her lips to hang down. And she was blowing through them. She had become cream-colored and damp to the touch.

Sent to the hospital a couple weeks ago because her cancer apparently had metastasized, she had been sent back a few days ago to die. But she had looked fairly well as recently as this morning.

"She won't take any more fluids," Terry said. "I'm afraid to try any more, she might choke."

Pat tried by suctioning up some water in a plastic straw with her finger, putting the straw to Anna's mouth and releasing some of it. But it just dribbled down her chin. Pat straightened up.

Terry said, "When do you think she'll go?"

"Shh." She never wanted anyone to say something frightening, even in front of a comatose patient. You really could not tell what they could hear.

Terry whispered, "Is she Catholic?" Pat shook her head; they wouldn't need a priest. That was just about all she did know of her from her chart. Often, she knelt by her wheelchair and asked, "Anna, who is Uncle Josh? Did he raise you? Or is he someone you just loved very much?" But she would never answer, just call out to Uncle Josh.

She was on painkillers and, thank God, wasn't vomiting. Oxygen was available should she need it, not to keep her alive, but to ease her breathing should she start choking. The orders were not to try heroic measures, such as nasal feeding.

"Ter, dear, get me some glycerine swabs, please."

Terry came back with them, and Pat removed one from the pack and ran it around Anna's lips and inside her cheeks and on her lolling tongue. Then she went back to the station and called an official of the bank that was in charge of her financial affairs. Apparently, her husband had set this up in his will. She simply notified him that she thought he should know it probably would be over by tonight at the latest. Not that she expected him to come over, but he used to visit occasionally.

She went into the room several more times before her shift was over. Anna's limbs were turning cold. Here and there purple bruises had formed on her skin. On her last visit, Pat leaned over and kissed her on the forehead. Anna's roommate, a deaf-mute black woman, glanced over briefly as she walked by. She crossed herself.

The captain was standing near the door to the lounge. She stopped and said, "Captain, Martha's a very lovely person. Why don't you go with her once in a while? You might find you like to paint or build things."

"See."

"You do that. Well, I'll see you tomorrow. And you have yourself a good day."

She thought of him as she got into the car, maybe because it was easier to think of him than of Anna. He wasn't one of those patients you could joke around with or kiss. Certainly not kiss. And though she wished he would just ease up and be . . . well, part of things here, she rather respected the fact that he didn't. It was, she sensed, his way of standing back from really being here, for which she couldn't blame him at all. And, though he could be surly to the staff, she also respected him for the way he would talk up for the patients.

She sighed as she neared the outskirts of the city. She was suddenly tired, the day was finally hitting her. As she approached the countryside, though, she began feeling better again.

If there was one thing she could thank Warren for, and there was just one, it was the house.

Actually, she should either be called Mrs. Andreoli or Miss Lenkowski, not Miss Andreoli. She had kept her married name but somehow, probably because they didn't see a ring, people began calling her Miss Andreoli, and she finally yielded to it. But it was Lenkowski. She was born in a coal town thirty-seven years ago and was raised by her grandparents after her mother and father died when she was small, just a couple years apart. Maybe it was her love for her grandparents that eventually drew her into geriatric nursing; but she had long stopped trying to analyze it. They had been so wonderful to her; even though she was all they had, they had encouraged her to leave and go to nursing school.

For as far back as she could remember, she had wanted to be a nurse. And when she went into training—it had been a hospital school, not a college—she had been the stereotype of the wide-eyed small-town girl in the big city. When a medical student told her he loved her, and that this is what all people in love did, she'd had her first sex, in the front seat staring at a steering wheel. When he graduated and she never heard from him again, she thought she would get even by going out with a resident in pediatrics he had given her name to. That had been to a motel on the second date, and a number of residents and motels followed—until she turned off completely in disgust with herself.

Warren had been a patient when she worked as a charge nurse on a medical-surgery floor. On the fourth day, he asked her to marry him. Although a wise old director of nurses told her, dear, it's none of my business, but don't marry a patient until you get to know him for a long time, she had married him three weeks after he got out of the hospital. It wasn't long before she realized the mistake: he had married a nurse, someone he could be thoroughly dependent on, not a woman.

After taking those years of his drinking and rages and regrets, she finally had gone to a psychiatrist in the hospital who, on her first appointment, told her that her problem was that she lacked self-esteem, that she had a need to be maternal and thus was attracted to men who weren't worthy of her, whom she thought she could help. On the second appointment he came over to her chair and kissed her, and while she was struggling to get free was trying to unzip his fly. But the first visit had been worthwhile; she remembered the self-esteem part, and much of her believed it, and she was able to file for a divorce.

But it could be rough out here. She wished she were married again, had kids. Still, she just was not going to settle for the ones she could marry.

The captain had seen them pushing the bed. Though he had seen this several times before, it never struck him as unusual until now. He followed them, saw them turn into another hall, unlock a door there and start pushing the bed through. As he came closer, one of them waved him away.

So, that's where they kept the stiffs.

He went back to his own hall. For the first time in a long while he remembered not seeing certain faces any more. Where was Punchie, for instance? Beeno?

He got a little panicky because he couldn't remember. Then he realized he didn't even know what day it was. Remembering the sign they kept near the end of the hall, he walked over.

TODAY IS THURSDAY

He walked back to the room he thought they had come from. A curtain was drawn inside; he pulled it back and saw it concealed an empty floor.

Beeno? Punchie?

He didn't miss them, he was just afraid for them. And it was as if he had been lax, sleeping on the beat.

He looked into room after room but didn't see them. But he did see Josh Lady, whom he had forgotten about also. She was lying in bed.

Later, he saw Garbo and others going back and forth to her room. He could detect trouble. Though he hated people who crowded the scene of an accident or something, got in the way of you doing your job, none of these cuckoos were going up there, so he felt free to stand outside her open door a couple times, though the curtains were closed now.

When Garbo stopped to talk to him in the hall on her way out, he wanted to ask her about Josh Lady. But there was that recreational shit. She wasn't bad as far as these people went, some others weren't so bad either, but they would turn, they would all turn. Meanwhile, they were only trying to get Rosemarie and Ellen and that son of his off the hook.

He went to bed at ten but slept for only a couple of hours. He got up and put on his robe. He saw the jig nurse, Murph, at the station; the clock on the wall above her showed it was a little after twelve. He went out in the hall and Murph said, "Captain, is something wrong?" and he shook his head and walked down the hall to that room. The curtain was pulled back and he could see her in the hall light, her face grayish, her lips open but still. The sheet was moving ever so slightly.

"Captain, where are you going?" Murph had come up to him, but he shook his head and went into the room and sat on a chair by the bed. A sharp whisper from the hall: "Go back to your room."

He didn't move. After she came in and peered at her, Murph whispered again, "Go back to your room," but he still sat there and, finally, though he didn't look to see, he sensed that she was gone.

He sat looking at her face. Soon he drew the chair closer and took one of her hands and covered it with his.

When the nurse checked again at two, she found her dead, the captain, arms crossed on his lap, asleep in the chair.

The next morning after breakfast he took a pencil and some crumpled paper he had in his jacket and, sitting by the windowsill, wrote carefully: No one ought die alone.

One thing he had disliked about being a cop was all the paperwork. It had gotten him into the habit, however, even after his retirement, of jotting down some thoughts. He used to think maybe he would put them all together and make a book out of his life and all the cases he was involved in. But he didn't even know where those notebooks were anymore.

Now he glanced back at some of the notes he had made on the papers. One said: She cried when L said gone send you state and I pleaded with bitch. Another: Dont ever kick out old. And another: I believe in capitol punishmnt. A deterint.

14

Late Saturday morning he got a call from the charge nurse on Wing D that one of the patients had been having diarrhea for the past few hours, and did he want to prescribe something like Lomotil. If it had been a weekday and he had been at the plant he would have done this, then checked later to see how she was. Though he hated giving up any part of a Saturday, she had been having an unusual number of complaints lately and he felt he had better go over. He was glad he did, for he didn't like the sound of her breathing and she was too senile to say if anything hurt. He ordered her sent to a hospital.

About to leave, he checked his watch and wondered what to do. It was going on twelve. He didn't know if Andreoli was on, and asked himself what difference it made; but he did go back. No one was at the nursing station, and he went through some of the charts. She came from one of the rooms.

He said, "I was over on D and just checking if there are any problems."

"I can't think of anything special."

He looked at his watch again. "It's almost twelve. Join me for lunch?"

She seemed uncertain. "If you can give me a couple minutes."

He glanced at her occasionally as she busied herself at the station. She was one of the best-liked nurses here, warm, extremely capable. Still, the girls liked to talk, and he had heard about the marriage and that there had been at least two wrong guys in the past couple years, a gambler who rarely won, a salesman who went back to Hawaii and his wife. They walked to the dining room. All the tables were fours at the least. He found himself hoping no one would ask to join them.

"Sadie, what do you have today?" she asked one of the women from the kitchen who came over.

"Mushroom barley soup. Fried chicken and vegetables. Peas and carrots."

When she left, Pat said, "It sounds like a nice lunch. The food here is really good."

"Have you worked at any other nursing homes?"

"No. The first one."

"How long's that been?"

"I've been here . . . let's see. Seven-eight, seven years."

"Then I don't have to ask if you like working in geriatrics."

"I really do. Except, you know, once in a while I'd like to help deliver a baby. But I do like it, yes. It's what I prefer."

"Do you carry it home much?"

She looked at him strangely. "Did you think I was foolish that time?"

"Crying? God, no. I didn't like to see you hurting. But foolish? No, not at all. Cross out the question."

"No, I'm sorry. Sometimes I take it home. It depends. Sometimes —well, you must know—sometimes you can face the biggest tragedy and it doesn't get to you, and then some much smaller thing throws you completely. It's hard to say what gets you involved. Sometimes I tell myself I'm absolutely not going to feel a thing any more. But I don't know, things hurt at times, but I still think it's better to feel than not to feel. You're looking at me funny."

"I'm really not. That was very well put."

"Well . . ." She took a breath. "You know what has gotten to me? These murders. Sometimes someone will say something in back of me and I just jump. I know some of the staff have asked that they hire a guard."

"What did they say?"

"You know, 'We'll see.' We'll see, what? Someone else get killed here?"

Their soup and then their platters came. They ate silently for the most part, then when they were almost through he said, "Did I hear you breed dogs?"

"You may have, but I don't. I have three dogs but I don't breed them. They're mongrels. Also I have two cats, one of which is expecting."

"And all of this in an efficiency."

"Are you serious?"

"Of course not. I'm joking. Is it an efficiency?"

She laughed. "No, I've got a very nice place, sorta country-ish. In fact, country-ish. Two acres. Lots of trees. An old, old house."

"Well, you'll soon be delivering babies."

"Me?"

"Yes, your cat."

"She had her kittens under the house last time. And I suspect that's where she's going this time."

Over coffee, she asked if he liked working in geriatrics.

"Yes, but I don't think I would want it full time."

"What you're doing must be a nice balance."

"I think so. I guess."

"Were you always in industry?"

"No, I was in general practice for many years. Then I had what they called a mild heart attack and I said, 'Patients dear, I love you and I want to help you, but someone else is going to keep these hours, see you nights, get up early and make rounds.'"

"May I ask if you had to give it up?"

"No, I wanted to."

"You must have been . . . you must have felt down. I'm sorry, I shouldn't have said that."

"No, that's fine. But what made you think that?"

"It would have been perfectly normal."

"Well, you're right. After my coronary—I hate guys who say 'my coronary'—anyway, I wanted to blow out my brains. That's not really true. I wasn't suicidal. No, that's not true either. Let's see if I can get this straight. Well, it was a blow to me that I wasn't as all-strong and all-powerful as a lot of people thought, that I could get sick. And I did think of suicide. Not very seriously, but I did think of it. This might sound strange, but the only reason I didn't let myself think about it seriously was my children. I thought that would be a hell of a 'role model' to be."

"How old are they?"

"Well, for a guy who's only twenty-seven I don't know how to explain that my daughter is finished college and working in New York, and my son is going to law school. Which is to say I don't remember their exact ages offhand—Karen, my oldest, I think she's twenty-five. So, this happened eight years ago. I didn't want them to think, years later when the world wasn't as pure and shiny as they used to think it was, that the answer to being low is to blow your brains out. So, yes, I was low."

"You seem to have gotten over it beautifully."

"And here I thought you were perceptive."

She seemed to be waiting for him to go on. And he wanted to, but at the same time he didn't want to sound like . . . a cliché. And what he would say would be a cliché. The middle-aged, married man bit. The guy looking back on the young fellow who always dreamed of being a surgeon, and then went left instead of right at the crossroads. The guy who still occasionally wished he could have been a professor and had written great papers and textbooks and helped people live, not just keep them going in a human warehouse until they died. He wanted to tell her this because he felt she wouldn't look on it as a cliché or, even if she did, that it wouldn't matter. That she would take it all in and make it a part of her and feel she had to reach out.

Still, he didn't say it.

Nor did he say something else which he really felt. It was selfish not to, he realized, but he held it back. Andreoli, you give too much. And you give so much you'll take just about anything in return.

Sergeant Christy said from the doorway, "Lieutenant?" and when LaSala looked up he came to his desk. "Someone to see you. Those two people's son, the Leonards."

"I'm in."

Edward Leonard was a slender man of thirty-two, with none of his father's coarse features, whom LaSala had spoken to soon after he was assigned to the case. He had seemed calm then as he tried to come up with some clue to his parents' murder, but he was obviously distraught now.

"Lieutenant, I hate to bother you. I would have called but I was driving by here and I thought I'd see you in person. I don't know if you know this, but I'm still getting calls saying they're glad Mom and Dad are dead, they deserved to get killed. They say all kinds of terrible things and hang up."

"How long's this been going on?"

"Since right after it happened. I must have gotten a dozen calls."

"Have you reported this before?"

"Yes, I called the station house near us. Someone there, I don't know who, asked me was it always the same person. I said at least two of them weren't, they were women. He said he'd try to do something about tracing the calls, but I never heard anything."

"Are the calls to your home or work or both?"

"Home."

"We'll contact the phone company and see about checking your calls. Chances are they're just nuts. It happens all the time. Have you gotten any letters?"

"No."

"If you do, call me, I'll want to see it. Look, what can I say? There are a lot of crazy people in this world."

Leonard's eyes grew wet. "Lieutenant, my mother and father were great people. The goddamn Alliance and the newspapers, they killed them. They're directly responsible. My father, they made him out like he was—he was—but he was a good person. He didn't do anything illegitimate. The court found for him. Would they have found for him if he was wrong? I'm sorry. I really am. Look, I just wanted you to know about the calls."

"There's nothing to be sorry about. Let's see what we can do. Easy to say, but try taking it easy. They're nuts. Just remember that. They're nuts." He walked him to the door, then came back to his desk. It was hard to admit, even to himself, but he had looked on the father as a heavy in this, had felt that the only two really innocent ones were the wife and the nurse. But even if he was a heavy, that didn't call for getting blown away.

At this point, they couldn't be further from closing it up. They had found the two people who had appointments with Leonard that night. They had easily come up with the man who had called about the nursing home unloading his mother. They had spoken to other families whose people got dumped. They had questioned most of the people in the Alliance. And, unless they had overlooked something, everyone was clean.

The only one they hadn't found yet was the soldier, and all the tips they had picked up said he had gone straight to Canada before the Latimore murder. As for tracing the .38—hoping it was registered—he wished that one on the Russian secret police.

And all the while, this was the kind of case that rarely just went bye-bye. These crazies didn't stop until you stopped them.

He was taking certain things for granted, the captain realized, and that was always a mistake. And what he was taking for granted was that it was really the nurse's car, not a family car; that she brought it in all the time.

In fact, all he could remember about it was that sticker. If they pulled that off, he was lost. He didn't know the make of the car; he wasn't even sure any more of the color.

He drifted out after dinner. But there was no car with that sticker. Maybe, though, it was her day off. The next morning and all through lunch he was nervous, waiting for three-to-eleven to come on. And when they did, he went out again, looking around the ground as though for something he lost, but glancing about. There it was: LOVE A NURSE TODAY. A green Buick.

Not new, not old, but it looked like a fast job. And it probably would be out there most nights if he needed it.

He sat on the veranda, feeling relaxed, but it became too hot after a while and he returned to his room. He became aware, then, that he hadn't seen Elephant Ears all day. He rarely said more than three sentences a week to Elephant Ears, and then only to ask if he wanted something. Elephant Ears had never even said that to him. But Elephant Ears was always around, and now he wasn't around. Simply gone like Punchie? Beeno? He went to Reds at the station; she had taken over three-to-eleven full time. "Where's the guy in the room?"

"What room, Captain?"

"My room, my room."

"He left. But he's all right. Don't worry about him."

"Where's he?"

"Captain, he's fine, he's with his family."

Bullshit. Nobody ever visited him.

He asked Talk-Talk, but Talk-Talk said, "Do they tell you anything around here? They don't tell you anything. You can ask a million questions they don't tell you anything."

He even stayed up for eleven-to-seven, but Murph without even looking at the chart said, "He's fine, he really is. Why don't you get yourself some sleep, honey?"

Don't honey me, you bastard!

He went back to his room. He stared at the empty bed. Elephant Ears was a stiff, he was in that room, they brought his bed back. Maybe he wasn't dead, maybe he really was with his family. Christ, somebody tell him something. He didn't care if he was dead as long as he *was* dead. But he didn't want to think he was dead if he was alive. And he didn't want to think he was alive if he was dead.

Something seemed to be spiraling fiercely in his head.

Bastards, you bastards, you better tell me something!

15

The first thing in the morning he strode over to Garbo. "Where's the guy in my room?"

"Mr. Silverstein? Didn't anyone tell you?" She tried to be as honest as possible with the patients, and this bothered her. "He had to go back to the hospital. He has diabetes, you know, and they think it may be affecting the circulation of his other leg. He's gone to a very good hospital and I'm sure they're going to take care of him fine."

He grunted as though it didn't matter, but he wasn't breathing as hard now as he stood by a window, looking out. He thought briefly about those ears, that sucked-in-face, but then lost himself watching the rabbits in the hutch. He wandered up the hall, thinking there were a couple new faces around, then, sure, this was a new guy: he was sitting stiffly in a regular chair, real silky white-haired and all decked out: he had on a hound's-tooth jacket with leather on the elbows, and pants a color that went with it. He even had on a clip-on bow tie. He smiled broadly at the captain as he went by. "Good morning."

He sounded clear-o, though you could never tell. Still, the captain avoided the clear-o's as much as the loonies, as if accepting them was like accepting the place. When he walked back later, Sporty was still there. Again that smile, again good morning.

After lunch it was good afternoon.

He wondered if he was like Talk-Talk. Both clear-o and nuts.

"Good evening." Christ, was he the official timekeeper? This time he was sitting in the lounge, held out his hand. The skin was covered with brown marks. The captain took it, dropped it.

"I just came this morning. Did you see me with my daughter, my Ruthie? My daughter brought me. She rides beautifully, and her children ride beautifully. She won twelve championships and I don't know how many seconds. My wife used to ride beautifully, too. She died. A day doesn't go by I don't think of her. But I've been living with my daughter and son-in-law at the house. I turned over my business to them. We manufacture golf balls. But I used to ride up until six years ago. I am eighty-one. Do you ride?"

He felt like saying yeah, the Number Eight trolley car. Old Sporty went on: "You'll see her tomorrow. My daughter's coming tomorrow. I wear a pacemaker. Did you ever feel a pacemaker?" He touched his chest. "And of course I always have to wear this bag," touching his side. "I'm not too steady on my feet, that's why I have this," and the captain noticed the pronged aluminum cane for the first time. "But this is a very, very nice place. And you'll meet my daughter tomorrow."

Fortunately, Old Sporty began talking to someone else, with that same big smile, and the captain was able to saunter off. He reminded him of another rich guy, Joseph Raymond Hester, that name was so clear to him, who bashed his wife's head in and only got three years. The main thing he had against Old Sporty was that Hester only got three years.

He was tired and beginning to yawn, and he decided to go back. As he went past Reds, he thought of Garbo and how he would just like to touch, nothing real fresh, you know, just like to touch her ass. There wasn't a single other person in this whole goddamn place whose ass he would touch. And he hadn't even thought of hers until today, sometime after she had told him about Elephant Ears and she had walked by him. He would just like to put the palm of one hand on one of those cheeks. Feel it in his palm and press in slightly and let go.

In bed, he thought of it again; then he thought of her coming in one day and saying Captain, how are you, let me make you feel better, massaging his chest, just massaging his chest and his belly and then down there, and then saying yes, Captain, you can kiss me here and opening her blouse as she leaned over him and letting him suck.

He hadn't thought of a woman in this way for months and months, maybe even years. Most of the nurses were fat asses or just mean behind those smiles and hello dears and how are you dears. And those poor, poor old bags in their wheelchairs, sitting with their legs apart and their skirts up to here and their pants or scraggly little businesses showing made it all the more wonderful that he loved touching her ass and sucking. Just that, no more, that was all he wanted, that was all, he wouldn't hurt her or think anything bad; but he had to stop thinking even this, for a part of him suddenly wondered, as he used to wonder as a kid, if the dead could see you from the sky. Not only see you but know all your thoughts. He thought of Josie looking on and felt ashamed, and made it all go away. Instead, he saw as clearly as he saw the moonlight on the window Josie and him talking in their living room only a year or two before she died. "Josie, don't you ever die on me first. I couldn't tie my shoes without you." "Oh, you'd have another woman two weeks after the funeral." And when she had died, sitting up in bed all at once in the middle of the night and then falling back, not a sign of sickness before, people said to him what they had once said to his mother about how only a good person dies without suffering. Nor had he understood it with Josie, the thing he understood now.

He wondered, if he had gone first, would they have put Josie in one of these places. He was sure they would sooner or later.

Though it was a sin to hate your children, he hated them more because they would have even put Josie away.

The next morning he felt some shame looking at Garbo. She had Talk-Talk sitting quietly over by her station most of the morning, something that got him slightly annoyed at Talk-Talk for some reason. Old Sporty, still wearing that outfit and smiling, said good morning to him, he would be sure to introduce him to Ruthie today. By afternoon, though, Old Sporty had moved to one of the windows in the lounge, was peering out with a hand shielding his eyes. And by dinnertime, the captain noticed, he was no longer smiling.

The captain kept glancing over at him as he ate. It was like seeing someone who'd been killed or beat up or robbed, and hating whoever out there did it. The do-gooders, they didn't know that feeling, had never seen anyone with a breast ripped off or a mother and father crying in each other's arms or someone who couldn't make a cent anymore screaming about their life's savings.

He'd pull her in by the hair if he could!

He couldn't even relax enough to watch TV.

"Hey, what's this?" He had gone back to his room and now was shaking in rage at the station. "Where's my stuff?"

"Captain, I'm sorry, I forgot to tell you, I was busy," Reds said. "You're in Room 203 now, we need your room. We're having a man and wife come in in the morning and we need a double. But you're in a beautiful room now, I think it's better than the other."

He went there, dazed.

Reds came to the doorway. "We even gave you the window. You don't have a roommate yet, so we automatically gave you the better bed."

He sat down on the bed. If he didn't, he knew he would leap at her.

"You don't get the direct sun here, which is a definite advantage," she said.

He stared at the doorway long after she was gone. Not even to ask? Or to say they were going to? Too busy? Fuck too busy!

I'm a human being!

But that made it worse. It made him Talk-Talk.

He lay awake most of the night, didn't drop off until nearly dawn. When he woke, Garbo was standing by his bed. "I don't want you to miss breakfast. Or don't you feel well? Do you want breakfast brought in?"

He shook his head.

"Well, I see you're in a different room. Oh, and you're going to have a roommate today. He was here before but he had to go to the hospital, he had a stroke. His name is Henry Lynch. He can't talk, he had an operation several years ago for cancer of the mouth and throat. By the way, and this is important, if you prefer someone else we'll change later on. But right now we're full."

He barely heard her. He was still thinking that they hadn't even asked, just packed his stuff.

"Well, I'll leave and let you get dressed."

Lynch turned out to be the poor guy he had thought of to worry the albino. No Voice. His chin and part of his throat were gone. Always gave him the willies. They had to lift him off the litter onto the bed.

Not to ask, not to say anything. He carried that around with him all day like a recording.

It was just starting to ease up the next day when he saw the newspaper story.

LaSala saw it also. An investment broker named Shoyer had just been released from prison after serving less than a month of a ten-to-twenty-year sentence for swindling dozens of elderly people in a stock scheme. The appeals court had found a number of things wrong with the indictment and ordered him released and retried. According to the story, a key witness had disappeared.

LaSala took the paper into Captain Denny's office and had him read the story. Denny looked up. "If you're thinking what I'm sure you're thinking, you're right. He's a target."

"Put a watch on his home?"

"At least. But you have to let him know. He might say we're harassing him. And that could help blow his trial. If he's ever going to have one, that is."

"I'm not all that wild about protecting this guy."

"It's not protecting him, it's the city. Let me talk to the inspector."

He came back from McDowell's office. "O.K. But you have to clear it with Shoyer."

LaSala called him and made an appointment at his home, a large Tudor house just inside the city. Shoyer, a bulky man who kept putting on and removing his glasses, said, "You're scaring the shit out of me, you know. Where would your men be?"

"Here at the house. We'll work out where, the hours. Do you have an office?"

"After what they did to me? I'm out of business." He thought. "You know, I'm not guilty. This is like saying I am guilty. I don't like it at all."

"It's all up to you."

"No, I don't like it." He began to grimace. "But I better do it for the family."

16

The captain woke to the sound of voices and machinery outside, then saw from his window that they were digging up some huge old tree stumps near the parking lot. He stood outside and watched them most of the morning, glad that something different was happening around here. It wasn't until during dinner that it began worrying him. What if they'd had to move the rock? Found the keys?

Outside, he walked slowly along the parking lot. All the rocks looked alike but he knew that his was exactly the eighth one from the end. He had memorized that number very carefully, had even marked it down. He was counting to himself now, but wasn't sure if he had counted one rock twice, and he counted again. He went over to it, glanced around, then bent down quickly. Just a fast little lift was enough.

He walked back to the steps. He had been planning on going tonight, yet in a way he was glad she hadn't showed up today. When it came right to it, he was nervous about using the car. But he would use it.

A foot up on the steps, he was staring out the driveway at an ice cream truck with a large cone on the roof that was stopped at a red light. Across the street some children were waving at the driver. He watched the truck pull over.

He had forgotten about ice cream trucks and the bells and kids cluttered around, waving coins. It called back to mind so many neighborhood streets, and even being on the beach with his kids and a guy in white lugging a box on his back and "Pop, can we have money, can we have money?" He walked down the driveway and leaned against one of the stone walls and just watched. It was driving away now, and the kids were slowly scattering. He looked at the store on the corner with a sign that said J & D Appliances. He walked over and looked in the bright window, at the TVs, the radios, the washing machines. Next door was a hardware store. He used to love working with power tools, though he never really had the time to give it.

Men's clothes next, but he was never much for that. Bridal gowns, and he thought of Rosemarie and Ellen. And Josie, how could he have forgotten Josie in her gown and, geez-o, that picture where she was holding flowers and his chin was so high because of that stiff collar? The kids used to haul it out of the attic once in a while just to laugh. A closed luncheonette; keep a nightlight on in there, fellow. A sign said "Electric Shavers Repaired," and the word shavers became Shoyer for an instant, but not with that burning feeling anymore. An upholstery shop, then across the street a drugstore that seemed big on trusses; it was closed, too, and he had the feeling he would like to check the door. Now the barred window of a darkened pawnshop.

"Captain?" Someone put his arm through his: a big blond orderly. A car was at the curb. "We have to go home, Captain. Getting dark."

He yanked his arm away. "Don't grab me!" But he was flustered. What was wrong?

"We have to go home, Captain. It's getting dark."

"So?" He saw the albino behind the wheel. What the fuck was this? He was just taking a walk.

"Come on, Captain. Time to go back."

"I can walk back!" It was like he was a crook you jump out and grab on the street.

"I know you can. But let's ride."

He let himself be eased over to the car, suddenly afraid of trouble. When they arrived back at the home one of them walked with him to the wing, then went ahead and spoke to Reds while he watched. One of the words he heard was "wandering." She came over to him. "You scared us, you know that? If they didn't find you we were going to call the police. You know what time it is? It's going on nine. Now that was bad. That's really bad. That's not at all like you. Now, you go in and get undressed. I want you in bed."

He got into pajamas, robe, and slippers. No Voice, who watched him as he came in, had fallen asleep. The captain walked out into the hall but didn't like the way Reds was watching him. It was the way you watched a guy you thought might make a break for it in court.

"What're you lookin' at?"

"Why don't you just take it easy tonight, Captain?"

He went back into the room. He didn't want to see that ugly face. A guy seventy-six can't walk outside? He jumped up to yell something but made himself sit back on the bed. He pulled off his robe, flung it to the corner, dropped off his slippers, and lay back on the pillow, staring up at the ceiling.

He heard footsteps in the hall. He closed his eyes. If he saw that face he was sure he would snap; he had to save his anger, use it right. Don't ever blow your case on the little fish. The footsteps were here now. The light over his bed went off.

Then, almost in disbelief, he heard the bedrails go up.

He was too shocked to react for several moments. Then he reached through one set of rails to find what the hell locked it in place. But he couldn't find it. He began to shake the rails furiously, then stood up and started to climb over the side. But his foot caught on something and he tumbled over and fell to the floor.

The light flashed on in the room. Reds was bending over him, her freckles like pit marks on chalk. He pushed her away and got to his feet and started for the hall. "Captain, stop that!" And he did, not because of her command but because he realized he had nowhere to go. She circled around him and came back with the albino and the blond.

"Come on, Captain," she said, "back to bed."

He didn't move. He was too confused, shaken.

"Come on, Captain," the blond said gently. And he led him back to bed. The captain lay down heavily, then started to rise when he heard the rails going up again. Suddenly his wrists were grabbed, something was being wrapped around them; his arms were tied to the rails. He started to pull at them, then to kick.

"Stop that!" Reds shouted. It jolted him into lying still. "Captain, we're doing this for your own good. God knows what you might have done to yourself. I don't know if you broke a bone or not."

The possiblity that he had broken something scared him. He went limp. They stood watching him for a while. Then she turned off the light again and they left. He became aware, then, of strange sounds in the room. Little squeals. He realized they were coming from No Voice; he was trying to tell him something. Biting at his lips he began to cry.

When he woke in the morning he saw some faces hovering over him, saw them so hazily he instinctively knew they had given him something at night. He heard questions: does this hurt, how about this, what about here? And he would shake his head as they poked and squeezed, had him move his arms, bend his knees.

They helped him to his feet now and into a chair. His head drooped forward, his arms were on some kind of table. Soon he realized it was a tray, that he was in a wheelchair. They weren't putting him in no wheelchair like a crazy! He rose up and started to climb out of it. It began to teeter but there was a rush of people toward him, holding him in. When they moved back, he started to stand again but realized he couldn't. He was tied in now. Garbo was kneeling in front of him saying, "We're doing it for your sake, Captain, we don't want you to hurt yourself." But then there was Talk-Talk yelling, "Hey, Captain, welcome to the club. They got us beat, Captain, they got us all beat. It is a very depressing situation. They don't know we're human beings, they don't think we have any feelings."

He fought to stand up, started to lift the whole chair with him, then he dropped back.

No, that wasn't the way. He remembered what he had said to Yorky.

"When're you going to wise up? The more you bust out, the longer you're going to be in the can, you're only building up your time."

And so he forced himself to sit still, to look at them as if all his strength were gone. And neither that day nor the others that followed did he fight the restraints. He ate calmly, he went to bed quietly; and on Sunday he even asked could he attend chapel. Every Sunday a different church in the area, complete with choir, would be in charge of conducting services in one of the lounges. The captain had been a fairly regular churchgoer when Josie, God rest her soul, had been alive. Here he had come to chapel just once. Even then, standing against the wall and taking in the slack faces, the weighted down heads, he pushed off long before it was over. Now, he even sang all the hymns.

The following day, which was six days after he was put in restraints, Garbo came over and untied him.

He stood up slowly from the chair. He was a little weak. But soon, though his face never revealed it, he felt all-powerful, uncaged.

17

David had some free time after lunch and he used it to sign a death certificate. He decided to check on the captain while he was there. He had them put him on a tranquilizer when they'd called; and even though it was a low dose, and he had lowered it even more the last few days in restraints, he was always particularly concerned about possible side effects in the elderly. Much more so when they were on other drugs as well. Pat told him he seemed to be doing fine; did he want to look at him, he was in one of the lounges.

"No, that's all right. Look, let's cut out the tranquilizer—see how he does." He looked up at the clock. "I'm going to have to beat it."

"Hey, when did you get back from the moon?" It was Dr. Persky. He was hunched forward in the chair, chewing on a cigar. He was wearing a red baseball cap, which he lifted and put back on. "Look what they gave me. Supposed to make me happy. If it does 'em good I'll wear it. Give 'em what they want, I always said. Made me a great doctor. Never took out a hem-orrhoid anyone wanted."

"You love it, Doc," Pat called out to him.

"See that girl? I'd blow my brains out wasn't her. I'd wave goodbye and go skiddoo. You hear I got a son in Boulder, Colorado?" Yes, a hundred times. "You hear I got a daughter in Paris, France? Paris, France, I don't need, I don't need no frog doctors. But Boulder,

Colorado. 'Dad, we just moved out here. We'll send for you.' Oh ho ho! A year ago. I've always been an independent fellow. But a colectomy doesn't make you feel good. I'm seventy-nine. And the legs ain't good. But I'm a human being, I got feelings. I specialized in the behind but I knew people had mouths. I let them talk. I listened. See that girl? She listens. She says she'd marry me only I'm too young. An old joke, but you reach my age you even need old jokes. You know what a *kvetch* is? A complainer, a pain in the ass. Once you're known as a *kvetch* you stay a *kvetch*. I'm Dr. Kvetch around here."

"Doc, we love you," Pat said.

"I love you too, doll. That's something I never even said to my wife. That's a joke, too. I loved my wife."

"Doc, take care, I'll see you," David said.

But Doc was looking away, to one side, as though at something only he could see.

"O.K.," David said to her, "I'll be going. Hey. You look like the wrath of God."

"It's Mr. Heggens. He's only got the one daughter, you know, and she gets me so goddamn mad. She can't leave without saying, 'Dad, I'll see you tomorrow.' And he sits by the window every day, and of course she doesn't show up. I called her, I told her, 'Don't say you'll be in tomorrow if you're not. He's alert, he knows what you're saying.' But she says, 'I can't walk out like that.'"

"Let's see what I can do. I'll call her a little later."

"It just gets me so mad."

He watched as she pulled in a breath and then reached to pick up some papers.

"How about dinner tonight?" It simply came out.

She looked at him. Her face had reddened, she seemed confused.

He said, "I've embarrassed you. I'm sorry. That was very dumb and I've embarrassed myself."

"Don't be. Let me think." She continued gathering papers together. He saw her swallow nervously. Then, still looking down at the papers, she nodded slightly, quickly.

He was nervous all that afternoon, wavering between regretting it and looking forward to it. He had cheated only once on Laura, years ago at a medical society meeting, when someone bought a girl and he had gone reluctantly into the room with her and he felt so guilty he almost didn't make it. At most two seconds. But he had thought about it a lot since his attack. You only go around once. Live it up.

He wondered what to say to Laura. A medical society meeting. He was trying to think of names he would be with, when they were meeting, what time they would break up—all the things she was bound to ask. But she was busy with a customer, said enjoy.

He picked Pat up at her home, her dogs sniffing around his legs and leaping up at him as he walked from his car to the front steps. She came out before he reached the door. She was wearing a skirt and a blouse, her hair long and straight, a peach sweater over her shoulders and a red bandanna knotted at the side of her throat. He had never seen her without a uniform. He grimaced as she bent down and let each dog kiss her on the lips—the *lips*.

"Aren't you afraid you'll give them a cold?"

"What's that?" she smiled as she stood up. "Oh. Don't you like dogs?"

"Love them. But not what they eat."

"Oh that's silly. Nothing that loves you gives germs."

"What a great title for a song."

It had taken him a long while to decide where to eat. Then he had remembered a nice quiet restaurant about ten miles farther out from here; but now, only when he pulled into its lot, did the name hit him with any impact: The Hideout. They were given a table by a window overlooking a pond that even had ducks. He ordered a J&B and soda, she a glass of chablis.

"So," she said.

"I don't like that kind of language."

She laughed. Then she said, "I'm very nervous, you know."

"I am too."

She looked around. "This is very, very nice."

"It's got a great name too."

"You mean it's famous?"

"No, I mean it's got a great name."

"I didn't notice. What is it?"

"The Hideout." He had wanted to mention it before she did. But if she felt anything about it she didn't show it. He said, "I want to thank you."

"What for?"

"For having dinner with me."

"And I thank you too. But let's make an agreement. Just this once."

"Just this once. What time tomorrow?"

She smiled slightly. "Just this once."

"Let's start off with hobbies. You tell me yours, I'll tell you mine. You, let me guess. You collect old baseball cards."

"How did you know that? And you—I'm trying to think of something funny, but I have absolutely no sense of humor. I mean I *have* a sense of humor, but not in the sense of *saying* anything funny. Does that make sense?"

"Absolutely. What did you say?"

"You know, I never saw you smile before."

"I guess you never saw me at a deathbed."

"That's terrible."

"Seriously. You really never saw me smile?"

"I don't think so. I don't remember. But I've always looked on you as very serious all the time. And you're not."

"Well, maybe it's because I feel very good right now."

"I'm glad. And so do I." The waiter came with their drinks. She took a sip, put it down. "That's nice and chilled. Should we look at the menu?"

He watched as she studied it. He thought: she's so damn pretty. A silly word, but she was. And again he had that feeling that it would be easy to tell her all the clichés, that they would come as fresh and new. If there was any one thing he found hard to take about Laura it was that she couldn't seem to forgive him for bringing up anything unhappy; saw it as an attack on her, the marriage.

Pat took in the strays. Although he told himself what did it matter, he wished he didn't know about the other strays.

"See anything you like?" he said.

"Everything. I was thinking, I was thinking—veal piccanti."

"I'm going to have the brook trout. And I want you to know I'm going to be serious from now on. Completely and totally serious."

"Good." She imitated his serious expression. Then she smiled.

The sense of elation stayed with him all through dinner and most of the ride back, but as they came within a couple miles of her home he felt it slipping away. She apparently did too, for they had started talking about patients, as though they were two people standing by her station and not heading toward her home. The dogs were barking as they drove up the dark lane. He felt uneasy, telling himself not to try anything, maybe just a kiss on the cheek, nothing more, but just go, don't get involved. He braked the car, leaving the ignition and headlights on. "Thank you for a beautiful evening," she said. "Please don't get out. I'm going to go."

He put his hand on her shoulder and she shook her head quickly. "Good night, and thank you," and she touched his arm and then turned to open her door; but when he put his arm around her she came back, her cheek against his. He held her. Then he lifted her chin, and she said, "Don't," but didn't resist, and he kissed her. Then her arms slid around his neck for the first time, and she pressed her cheek to his and held on hard. He found her mouth again, his fingers through her hair. Soon he opened his door and came around and opened hers. She looked at him, then with him by her side walked to the house. She opened the door, and when she closed it he kissed her again, their tongues meeting and turning.

They walked upstairs and in the dark of her room undressed quietly. They lay side by side now; but all at once it was different. As they kissed he couldn't shake the awareness that he was in a strange house and it was late. He stayed aware of this even as he kept thinking how beautiful she was, how exciting this should be. But he felt nothing now except for the galloping of his heart. And he was suddenly afraid for his heart. He said, "I don't know what . . ."

She put a finger to his lips, then kept her arms around him, her head against his chest.

"Just hold me," she said. "Just hold me, just hold me. And let me hold you."

The captain had come in when they had been talking at her station, saw the color burst into her face, saw the way she looked after the doctor as he walked off down the hall.

He had been right all along. With all her sweetness and kissing and *words*—she was one of them.

18

The first thing he had done after being released from restraints was to go to his closet where he had put the section of the newspaper that carried the story of Shoyer's release from prison. When he didn't see it under the stack of underwear, where he was sure he had put it, he began flinging aside the clothes, taking out shoes, slippers, socks. Where the hell was it? He yanked out his night table drawer, thinking maybe he was wrong, maybe he'd put it there, but after pushing things aside and feeling all around he slammed it shut. He went back to the closet for another fast look, then stood up. He wondered had he actually left it on the bureau and they'd simply thrown it away. Or had one of the nuts been through his closet? In fact, he was sure he was missing some socks and that blue shirt.

What was that broker guy's name? But he couldn't remember it any more.

He went into the lounges, thinking maybe they had saved some of the old newspapers. But he only found that morning's. He tossed it back on the table, trying to think what to do. Maybe it was out in the trash. He started to go outside but then stopped; he felt that an aide was eyeing him.

He had to go easy for at least a few more days. The word was out on him: he's a nut, he wanders.

How could he find the name, the address?

He went back and got today's newspaper again. He looked at the front page carefully but after several pages he began losing patience and turned them faster. He found nothing about Shoyer, but on the first page of the second section he saw a picture of the commissioner of police and a caption that said they didn't have any new leads to the murders.

Every time he saw the Pistol's picture he wanted to put his fist through it.

The cops themselves hung the name on him years ago because he was too much even for most of them. They used to say there were ten reasons the Pistol would shoot a guy, and the first one was sneezing.

One of the worst things the captain remembered was the time that poor old crazy jig barricaded himself in the second floor of his house. He would stand up and brandish a rifle over his head and duck low. The Pistol headed up the old Third Precinct then but he wasn't in when the alarm came and his men were just looking up at the window from behind their cars when the captain and his boys were called in as backup. And it was right just to wait, because he hadn't fired a shot and friends were looking for his wife and sons and his minister. But then there's the Pistol pulling up and his face becomes blood when he sees the captain, and there he is talking to one of his men, and there they go into the house, each with a twelve-gauge riot gun. And then that terrible blast from inside.

Later he had gotten the Pistol in a small room. Though the Pistol was some twenty-five years younger, same rank, the captain had grabbed him and said, "You killed him for no goddamn reason, you son of a bitch! I'm gonna see you up on charges!" But when he had gone to the commissioner about it he was told to drop it. The department wasn't encouraging jigs with guns.

And the Pistol, who was no longer the Pistol because the guys loved him now for pushing through all those raises and approving heavy hands, was the commissioner when the captain reached sixty-five. And even though the newspapers and even the city council urged that he be kept on for a few more years, the Pistol told him one word: "Pack."

The Pistol could be mayor, governor, even president of the whole United States, and he just might be some day, he was still a killer.

And for him to say that *these* were murders!

These!

The captain had given some thought to the possibility that he might have been mistaken about that look, but Benny had been in yesterday and he saw it on her again.

A look might fool him once but no way twice. In fact, how many times did he used to see someone drive by and there was something on a guy's face—maybe the way he looked at you or didn't look at you; it was hard to say what—but there was something that told him: that's a bum. And most times it would be a stolen car or there was a gun or a kid was leaving home. He couldn't remember all the times.

It was easy to tell today was a Sunday. Visitors were in the rooms, the lounges, kids were crying they wanted to push the wheelchairs. Sporty was sitting by himself near the front door, watching it. He was still wearing the bow tie, but the pants and jacket were crumpled. The captain went to a window, stood with his back to him, then came over.

"Hearda Jonah Powell?"

"No."

"Biggest singer, actor in the country?"

"Oh."

The captain was flustered. "Friend of mine." He walked away. Try to talk to a guy. Didn't know Jonah Powell. And sitting there waiting for his daughter. If he wasn't a little leery about making it two from here he would pull the switch on her himself.

John Kennedy himself had introduced him to Jonah Powell. Kennedy had been running in the primaries when he came to town to make a speech and the captain and some of his men were assigned to guard him. Then Kennedy met Jonah Powell out in Hollywood, and Jonah said he would be singing here at Convention Hall, and Kennedy said don't let anyone but Captain Hughes be in charge of security. After that he was always with Jonah when he was in town. Jonah even had him and Josie out to Hollywood, gave him a star sapphire ring, had him out to the set, introduced him to guys like Sinatra. He even remembered the first thing Sinatra said. "What's a cop doing in bad company?"

If he ever got around to writing his life story, a large part of it would be about Jonah Powell. It wouldn't only be about all the collars.

"Hey, Captain."

He looked around as he was nearing the door to the wing. It was Yorky and, behind him, Victoria. He had worried briefly that Yorky might have connected giving him the car that night with the headlines in the paper. But though some of that came back now, it disappeared quickly when Yorky said, "We stopped in just to say hello. We figured you might like a ride. How about a ride?"

He shook his head.

"Why not? Come on, it'll do you good. Vickie, tell him."

"How about a ride, Captain?"

He didn't know why he didn't want to go; just that something seemed to be tying him here, as if he would miss something if he left. But they kept asking, and soon he just shrugged his shoulders and let them sign him out. He was glad, once they drove out of the city and into the country, along winding roads where horses and cattle grazed behind fences. He rarely said anything; sometimes it became hard for him to think of words. But the clean air, in the way that anger seemed to do, cleared his mind. And, just as it happened at Rosemarie's house, the executions weren't . . . *quite* executions. He heard himself say, "Yorky?"

"What, Captain?"

"Let me live with you."

"Aw, Captain. Geez."

"Let me live with you, Yorky."

"Vickie, you hear that? You hear what he thinks of us? Captain, you're breaking my heart. We don't have room, Captain. You saw our place."

"I got a pension. I get Social Security. Get an extra room."

"Captain, your kids won't like it. They'll think we're out for your dough... Look. Let me and Vickie think it over. And if we decide yes, we'll call your kids. We can't do it without talking to your kids. O.K.?"

He nodded. He was breathing easier, having gotten it out. A few horses were peering over a fence. He liked seeing that. Later they stopped at a small luncheonette and had ice cream.

Yorky lowered the giant teeth of the crane until it was poised directly above the iron beams on the ground, then eased it down. It wasn't one of those big, big babies, the skyscraper kind, but at least he had a crane again. Now, at a wave from one of the men, he lifted the beams high, then swung them over and then down gently on the beams on the flatbed truck.

Out here, in the sun or the cold or the rain or whatever, you felt alive, good, and you knew if you slipped up you could drop iron on a guy's head. It was a job that required skill.

It was easy to put a gun to a guy's forehead and say give me. But this required a man.

How could he forget that debt?

His day done, he tossed his hat into the car and slid in, barechested, tan, sweaty. Last night both of them had kept saying it's up to you, but this morning Vickie just came right out and said let's do it: they would use part of his money to rent a larger apartment, part for his food. But when he dies? We'll still be able to afford it, Vickie had said; we can really afford it now; we'll have a TV room.

She was right. He was wondering, though he never mentioned it, if she was thinking the same thing that was in his mind: maybe he'll leave us some dough. He doubted if she would ever think like that; she wasn't like him.

His own thoughts worried him. He didn't want to take him in if he was doing it because he wanted his money.

By the time he reached home he had it worked out. If the captain left them any money when he died, that would be an extra. It wouldn't be why they were doing it, though. First, he didn't know if the captain had any money to leave. Second, he didn't know if he would leave it to them anyway. Third, he himself might zonk out first; him or . . . geez, God no . . . even Vickie.

Mark Hughes was tired when he came home. A lot of his friends thought he had a cushy job; after all, the bank closed at three. As manager of the branch he might have to work up till four, they conceded, but never longer than that. And he really couldn't convince them otherwise.

"Hello," his wife called from upstairs. "How are you?"

"Fine. How're you doing? Where's Timmy?"

"Riding his bike. Look, I'm almost in the shower. Someone called. There's a message by the phone."

Looking at it, he wondered who John Yorky was.

He dialed the number. "Is this Mr. Yorky?"

"Yeah. This Mr. Hughes?"

"That's right. What can I do for you?"

"Look, I don't know if you remember me, but I did meet you at your Mom and Dad's house some years ago. Anyway, I'm a friend of your father's. He gave me a lot of help when I was in a jam. I've been to the nursing home and he's been here. Like I say, I owe him a lot. Anyway, he asked me and my wife something yesterday, and I want to put it to you. He asked if he could live with us. We've been thinking about it and we decided that if it's all right with you it's all right with us. We wouldn't do anything without telling you first."

Mark was grimacing. "Wait, wait. Let's start from the beginning. How do you know my Dad?"

Several minutes later he had Rosemarie on the phone. "I told him no, of course. But Rosie, this is serious. It's not just a question of this guy taking Pop for his pension, his Social Security. Pop's got savings, he's got insurance, he can change his will at any time."

"Not if we get him ruled incompetent he can't."

"Rosie, it's not that easy. I know something about that. You need doctors to examine him, he can have a lawyer, there's a hearing in court. He knows where he is, I think he knows who the president is, he knows the day. You'll never get him ruled incompetent. Or there's a good chance you never will. But you can get him sore. And if he wins the case and he's sore, he might think to change it."

"Will you stop yelling? I can hear you."

"Who's yelling?"

"You're talking loud. Take it easy. We've got to be smart. So let's think. Let's think this out."

Rosemarie showed up at the home the following morning, found him sitting alone in the lounge. She kissed him on the cheek quickly, then lit a cigarette and sat across from him, crossing her legs.

"What's new, Pop?"

He said nothing.

"Look. This Yorky called Mark yesterday. Pop, why are you doing this to us? This is the best place for you. Wouldn't *we* keep you if this wasn't the best place?"

He looked at her silently.

"Pop, he's a crook. He's a jailbird. He'll take every penny from you."

"I'm goin' with them."

"Oooh, no you're not. Mark told him the score, and I called him afterward to make sure he really *heard* the score. Pop, don't make us do something we don't want to do. But the way you're acting we have no alternative. We can have you ruled something, Pop; I don't even want to use the word, but we can have you ruled that. We don't want to, you hear? But if you're going to act like an infant we're going to have to treat you like an infant. Do you hear me? And do you understand? Nod your head or shake your head; do something, don't just look at me! Do you understand?"

He couldn't help it, he nodded quickly. "Oh Pop," and she came over and tried to kiss him again but he pushed her away. He got up, fighting against smashing her face in, and strode toward the wing. She followed only part of the way.

Walking down the hall he saw Sporty sitting by his window. He wanted to go in there, shake him—Fuck 'em, fuck 'em, fuck 'em! Instead he went to his room, slapped both hands against a wall.

He had forgotten exactly why he had wanted to get out—it had to do with something more than just being out of here, he forgot what. All he knew was that he was glad he had tried, that it was important for him to have tried, but that he was just as glad he had failed. Out there, what was there for him to do? Here he had a job.

About ten o'clock Saturday night, LaSala met his wife after work at the Goldners. She was there with Sid's wife; Sid was supposed to have been home by now but was still on the street, had called to say he would be home in an hour.

LaSala drank some beer, watched TV, let them talk girl talk.

He had learned long ago that he felt more comfortable being out socially with other cops and their wives. He had other kinds of friends, but not many, and none close at all. The thing was, you never knew when you would get a little jab, maybe innocent but still a jab. Maybe they would ask about a story in the newspaper about police corruption or a cop on the take. Or what do you think about demonstrations? Or do you get sore when you hear "pig?"

Who needed it? It had gotten to the point that when he was at a party where there were strangers and someone asked what he did for a living he would say salesman or something.

He felt a little guilty that he was home while Sid was still out, even though he'd been in the office at six in the morning. And he couldn't get rid of the tightness in his gut, the quiet burping. He forgot how it was when he was younger, if he always got as tense as this, questioned himself as much.

He shouldn't question himself on this decision. It was the only one that made sense. And Captain Denny agreed.

It was two weeks since the first story appeared about Shoyer. And in that first week, LaSala had also assigned men to two other guys who made the papers. One owned a boarding house for the elderly that was cited for health and safety violations, the other was a teenager out on bail for mugging an elderly woman.

But he couldn't keep this up forever. He'd had to pull them off.

19

The wedding was held on their grounds, under a clear blue sky. And after the ceremony Carol Dodman stood with her husband and daughter and new son-in-law and his parents in the reception line under the trees that shaded them from the bright sun. She accepted the kisses and congratulations, now and then pausing to squeeze Lawrence's hand with joy. Afterward she hugged her daughter again and said, "Didn't I tell you the weather would be beautiful?" and she did a little something to Rina's hair and gown, then leaned forward for a hug from someone who had not made the line. The five-piece band was playing near the pool, the bar was busy, and waiters were moving among the crowd with trays of hors d'ouevres. The tables with their rose centerpieces and shiny white tablecloths and expensive silver were each shaded by a white umbrella. A few couples were already dancing.

She went over to Sally Strum, the *Sun-Journal*'s society editor, and thanked her again for coming.

"Why would I ever miss this? It's really magnificent, Carol. Your daughter looks beautiful, but she doesn't have a thing on Mama."

"Having passed that terrible age that begins with 'f,' I accept all compliments."

"Nothing terrible begins with 'f,' sweetheart," Sally said, and they both laughed. "Excuse me, I have to keep an eye on the photographer. He's an artiste, and if I leave him alone he'll only take pictures of the flowers."

Carol began mingling. When Lawrence came up to ask if she would like a drink she said not now, she was high as is.

She tried not to think about him as she made dinner. She had been thinking about him more than she should and it had to stop. Even the fact that they'd just held onto each other, kissing gently now and then, only added to him. She saw him as sensitive to so many feelings, to guilt, doubts, and she had never thought of him as sensitive before.

But she mustn't see him again.

Still, when the phone rang she picked it up quickly. Usually it is never the person you want it to be. Tonight it was.

They were driving past the motor camp now, then the outdoor movie, and around the curve in the road would be the long bridge over the bay. The bay was a rich glittery blue, dotted with boats and fringed with clapboard houses on pilings. He slowed up as they entered the island. When he reached the main road through it he turned left because that had always been his favorite part; it was quiet there, especially on a weekday.

He hadn't been here in years, and she had never been here. He had been looking forward to seeing it again, even more for her to see it. But the moment he made the turn and saw the kids jumping on the trampolines in the small amusement park, he wondered if it had been wise. He could still picture Karen and Jeff on them. He remembered how he and Laura would bring them here and sit with them on that wooden bench—there was still a wooden bench—and wait until the man in the booth called their names over the loudspeaker, "Karen B. take number three, Jeff B. number six." And a little later, "Three and six your times are up."

They used to spend at least two weeks here every summer. Twice they had a place for the whole summer, once facing the ocean, once the bay.

Pat said, "I see why you love it."

Over there was the miniature golf course, and there the several custard stands. And that great Italian restaurant, only it had a different name now, and the clam bars and the occasional gasoline station, then all the pastel cottages. He drove to the tip, only about four miles, and they sat watching the fishermen on the little dock there. He said, "There used to be a place up here where you could change. Lockers. I was sure it was up here, but maybe the other end."

But he didn't want the other end. They could change in the car but he hated that sandy feeling afterward, and he looked for a house that might have a sign that said "rooms." He passed several, but he recalled a place right on the beach that used to let them rent a room for the day. He drove there, a gray frame boarding house with an open porch in the front that was lower than the dunes. He rang the bell and a woman answered. "Are you the owner?"

"No, I'm her sister. Wait a second."

Her sister came and he said, "Could you rent us a room just to change? We have our own towels."

"Well, I got a little thing on the second floor. No bath, but there's a bath in the hall or you could use the showers out back."

It was a tiny room, with a sagging bed, a few chairs, a sink and a metal cabinet for a closet. He said, "As you can see, I spare no expense." They changed into swim suits, their backs to each other as though they had never been naked to each other before. He nodded his approval at how she looked, then touched her chin and she lifted her face and he kissed her. She put her arms around him, squeezing. Then she tapped him, leaned back and smiled. "Let's go to the beach."

He got a blanket from the car and they walked along a path through the dunes. Only a few people were on the beach, just two or three in the water near the lifeguard. They put the blanket on the hot sand near the dunes. He lay on his side, watching her put on sunglasses, then she lay with her back against him, looking at the water. The surf was rough, loud. A child came bellying through it on a little raft.

"That looks like fun," she said. "Did you ever do that?"

"Yes. The kids used to have them. Should I get you some lotion? You're very white."

"No, I'm fine. I really don't burn, I tan pretty quickly."

That morning, before picking her up at the house, he had stopped at the home to sign another death certificate. He found himself thinking of it, of the sights there. He touched at the sand. "Are you ready for some earth rocking philosophy? Enjoy life while you can. Deep stuff, eh?"

"It happens to be true."

"I was just thinking of the home. I really admire you. I'm sure I couldn't handle that all day."

"Then it's good you don't. And there's nothing wrong with that. I'm not so sure I could work with dying children."

"I just couldn't be around them all day."

"Them?" She looked at him with a little smile. She touched the tip of his nose. "Them, doctor, is us. There is no them."

"You're so right." He reached over and put his hand on her face. He brought her to him and kissed her, then looked at her and touched her hair. "You're really something, you know that? You are."

But she'd also made him think. Him in a home? If he was old, senile, impossible to handle, he wouldn't blame his kids for a second for putting him away. But let's say he was . . . fairly all right. Jeff would definitely put him away. Not Karen.

Not Karen? Who was he kidding?

"What're you thinking?" she said.

"My lousy kids. They just put me in a nursing home. And I shouldn't be there. I'm fine."

"At least you've got kids to put you away. The county's going to have to do it to me."

"And they've got their mother in a penthouse. And every time she thinks of where I am she begins to applaud."

"Jesus," she laughed, "you do have pleasant thoughts."

He thought: so much of my life I've spent feeling guilty. First about my parents, now about Laura and even the kids. And all the while those catheters are waiting.

"My husband didn't want kids," she was saying. "And I went along. Or maybe I didn't want the kids to have him for a father."

He waited for her to go on, but she didn't. He said, "Do you like it here?"

"Oh, my." Her head was on his stomach, she looked at the sky. "Tell me . . . let's see what. All right. Tell me about your father."

"My father? He was a druggist. Died when I was eighteen. My mother remarried and she died five years ago. I'm an orphan."

"Poor, poor orphan child."

"And your folks?"

"I'm an orphan, too. I was raised by my grandparents. My mother's parents. They were so great."

She lay there as though she were falling asleep. He touched just a wisp of her hair and she turned and smiled. "Feel like the water?"

"Let's go."

They went into the water once after that and remained on the beach until after five, when the lifeguard went off and only one other couple was left. The sea gulls seemed to know that the beach was completely theirs now, and they swarmed in with their sounds, landing for a while to waddle about and peck at the sand.

"Hungry?" he asked.

She nodded and they both stood up and shook out the blanket and folded it. While he put it in the trunk she went to shower. She came back to the room in a big towel and he paused on the way to the shower to kiss her lightly on the mouth. When he returned to the room the door was locked. He knocked, the towel tucked around him.

"Just a second."

She had on a blouse and panties, her hair wet and uncombed, her feet bare. He said, "Look out there."

"I have been. It's so beautiful."

They had a corner view of the beach. It was empty as far as they could see; a slight haze was coming in from the ocean. She stood with her back to him, looking out, and he put both arms around her. They stood for a while without moving, then he turned her and kissed her. Then he took her to the bed and, standing, unbuttoned her blouse and made her bare, then lay back with her on the bed.

"Just hold me," she said, for again there was nothing. But as he held her, his cheek against hers, he became aware of the very texture of her skin, the wet sweet smell of her hair, and with it his quickened breathing, a need to touch, to feel, to rub, caress, squeeze, to kiss, to explore. And now, mouth open, eyes closed, she awaited him, arching with one quick spasm as she took him in, then folded herself around him. And later, much later, they fell apart, then came close again, arms flung over each other, and slept.

20

Yorky showed up early one evening that week in his work clothes.

"Captain, I just want to tell you something. I don't want to hurt you about your kids but I got to tell you. I don't know if you know it or not, but I asked them about you coming with us and they said no. They gave me the feeling they think I'm after your dough. You know I wasn't after dough, Captain. You know that, don't you? They even said they don't want me to see you no more, I'm bad for you. I don't want this to bounce back on you in no way, but if you want to see me I want to keep coming around. Take you for rides. What's wrong with coming around? Taking you for a ride? . . . Captain, you hear me?"

He was thinking of something else, something he had never thought about before. "They ain't gettin' none."

"None what?"

"Dough. Nothin' from me. Not a goddamn cent!"

"Hey, come on, they're your kids."

"Nothin'! Nothin'!"

"How about a ride now? Come on. You eat yet? We'll get something to eat."

"No." He only wanted to be alone, to try to work this out. Yorky could tell.

"Captain, I'll see you real soon. I got you upset. I didn't mean to get you upset, but I didn't want you to think it was me and Vickie. And I wanted you to know—I didn't know what they told you—I wanted you to know I'm still coming around if you want."

With Yorky gone, he was trying to think of his lawyer's name. It was one of them Jewish names, Goldstein, Goldberg, something. He would remember if he just calmed down. A young guy, seemed nice.

Then he thought of something else: if he called the lawyer and told him I want to change my will, would he call the kids? After all, Mark was the one who got him. And if he did let them know, they would throw away the key on him.

He went back to his room and got a piece of paper from his night table drawer. He placed it on the windowsill and then, after giving it thought, began printing on it, pressing hard with his pencil.

> I WALTER HUGHES LEAVE ½ ALL MY MONY TO FRIEND JOHN YORKY AND ½ TO POLICE PENSHON FUND. DONT CHANGE THIS. THIS IS FINAL. I AM NOT CRAZY.

Then he signed his name very carefully.

In the morning, he looked at it again and it satisfied him thoroughly. After breakfast he remembered that you should have a witness. He thought about going to the office, but that would be as bad as the lawyer. He walked along the hall with the paper and saw Talk-Talk with the group in the recreational therapy room. He waited down the hall until Talk-Talk wheeled himself out. "Hey Captain! All that medical school to make a basket!"

"Sign this." He handed him the paper and pencil.

Talk-Talk didn't even look at it. "You crazy? I didn't sign nothing and look where the hell they put me! Where would this put me? China? Me sign a paper? Ho!"

The captain grabbed the paper from him and went to his room and stuffed it in the coat pocket with his other papers. He was angry but he couldn't blame him. How could he blame him? That's what they do to you.

A few days later he was desperately trying to reach Yorky, but by the end of the evening there was still no answer. He tried early the next morning, and in the afternoon, whipping the dial around furiously—but only those maddening, endless rings. He banged the receiver onto the hook, wondering again what to do. He had gotten the keys from outside, had them in his pocket, but he couldn't break through the worry about using the car. If he took it he not only would have to be back before eleven, but he had noticed one sleepless night that a nurse came in every few hours to touch No Voice's mattress in the dark, apparently to see if he had wet through again.

Back in his room he went through the route again. If the address was where he thought, it should be a few blocks off the road by the river. You took that cutoff there, he couldn't remember the name, but you took that cutoff and somewhere along there you came to Bowman, and the place would be either a few blocks to the right or left. He had been there many times years ago. It was no more than a half hour from here, if you didn't get lost.

Try Yorky again tomorrow?

He was so anxious to get to them that he hated to lose another day, even though he didn't know if he would find them there or if they had company or what. They had gotten away with it long enough. They didn't deserve to breathe another day's air.

Either way, whether he went tonight or waited to call Yorky tomorrow, he had to get the gun.

He put on his jacket.

The girl at the front desk simply looked at him, then back at her work. They trusted him again. He had learned the rules: they don't tie you up for shooting off your mouth. You could yell anything you want: "Hey, don't you hear him callin' from the room?" "Don't let her sit there wet!" "Give him a hand with the soup!" You could even add, "you son of a bitch." In fact, that sometimes made it funny, made them smile. They didn't tie you up for that or for dribbling from the mouth or dumping in your pants. Just don't swing a fist or kick. Or wander more than once.

Some of the ladies and gents, he saw, were out there on the veranda. They stared straight ahead or down, didn't seem to notice him or each other. Still, he shuffled past them, finding it hard not to try to run, to get around the corner of the building and see if the wood was still stacked the way it was and if anyone was around. No one was there, but he saw with anguish and anger that they had tossed on some extra wood, sawed pieces of the tree stumps they had dug out.

Dragging them off, he let them tumble down the pile to the ground. Occasionally, he would shoot a look over his shoulder. He lifted a large piece with both hands, let it drop near his legs, picked up another.

At last one opened up to the plastic.

He whipped the gun from it and jabbed it in his pants, pocketed the cartridges and then lifted the log and let it drop over the plastic again. He was completely out of breath, had to hold onto the pile until the gasping, the burning, eased. He turned around and his knees almost went. A woman was standing a few feet away, staring at him. She had coiffed blue-gray hair, glasses, a thin stern face, was wearing a flowered dress. He thought in panic: from the office: A visitor?

"Did you," she said, "see the children? They haven't come home from school yet."

It was then that he noticed she was picking at her fingers.

She reached out an arm as he circled around her. "Dinner will burn, and they aren't home."

He began walking away.

"But they're not home!"

He went straight to his room, then started to back out. They were lifting No Voice out of a wheelchair into bed.

"If you're going formal, Captain," Reds said, "we better press that jacket."

When they left he went to his chair by the window. He was exhausted, felt sure he would have to wait until tomorrow. He would wait about an hour and call Yorky again.

Soon he heard No Voice squealing, holding up the cord, indicating he had been pressing the button for a nurse. They kept a little slate and a box of chalk on his bed. With the one good arm he had left from his stroke he picked it up and wrote on it laboriously, then raised it. WATR.

"Water?"

A nod. He poured from the pitcher into a plastic cup, put a straw in it, which they always did, and No Voice took the cup and sucked.

It was like looking at a mutilated body, only it moved.

It was like kneeling by it in some field and thinking wherever you are, whoever you are, I'm going to get you.

"Daddy, take care of yourself," Josie used to say at the door sometimes. He would never say anything to that because you just couldn't promise.

Why should he try playing it safe now? Was that *him*? Those animals, they could be leaving the country tomorrow.

Clutching the keys tightly, he stood against the side of the building, looking over at the cars. He figured he had about two hours, but he didn't care. He just wanted them. They were murderers and he wanted them.

He wasn't sure that No Voice had actually been asleep. But he had made sure to put his will out on the night table. Even if it wasn't legal, the kids would know how he felt.

He tried to see the green car—he knew just about where it was, and he kept looking from car to car until he saw a bumper sticker. He couldn't read it but it was the only bumper sticker he saw.

If he just walked diagonally across the parking lot he would get to it. But he would be easier to spot from a window than if he ran across to the grass right here and then walked behind the cars, using them as a shield.

He strode across quickly and, hunched over, went from car to car. Then he remembered that the bumper sticker was on the other side. He stopped at the first car that looked green—he couldn't tell if it was a Buick. He slipped between the cars, turned the handle; the door was unlocked. He slid in. His hand was shaking so much he couldn't get the key into the ignition, or it was the wrong car. There, it went in.

He reached around in the dark to see where the hand brake was. He also found knobs, but wouldn't know until he turned or pulled them which one was for the lights. He didn't want to try now.

He turned the key and there was a long whining that burst into a roar. He backed out of the space, stopped, couldn't find forward for several moments, but had it now and was moving slowly toward the driveway. Nearing the street, he pulled one of the knobs and the headlights went on.

"No, I'm doing fine," Carol Dodman said into the phone. "Had a delicious shower, fixed my hair, am in my robe. So tell me. Do you think it's really an affair?"

"Well, she didn't come right out and tell me. But she did everything but."

"And it's one of the fellows who fixed her pool?"

"Are you recording this? I have to say everything twice."

"If you had to listen to what I'm listening to. I've got the bedroom door closed, he's downstairs but the goddamn stereo is so loud I can't hear you. Jesus, now it's the dog. Meg, let me call you back, will you? I've got to straighten this out."

"No, I have to run. I'll talk to you tomorrow."

"You are a bitch, you know that? I want to hear."

"Look, Howie's waiting for me."

"Well, just tell me this. Tell me you're sure it's an affair."

"I'm sure it's an affair."

"You are a sweetheart. I'll talk to you tomorrow."

She went to the stairs. "Will you turn down the goddamn music? Low! Low! And will you see to the dog? Jesus," she said to herself, and went downstairs. She walked into the den. He was asleep on the sofa. When she turned off the set he opened his eyes, yawned. "What do you want? Why'd you wake me?"

The barking of the dog stopped him as he got out of the car. Then the front door opened and a man was standing in the light, the dog barking by his legs. "What do you want?" he said as the captain walked toward him. The captain yanked out the gun and jammed it into his stomach, pushed him back into the house and kicked the door closed. Still barking, the dog backed away.

"Where is she?"

"Who?"

Then he saw her in the hall. She walked forward. "Who are you?"

He raised the gun and fired at her and then at him. He fell face down, but she was sitting on the floor, legs outstretched, a dripping rose above one eye. She swayed and toppled over. He stepped close and fired at her head again and then at his. He hurried to the door, started to turn the knob, then picked up a small throw rug and opened it with that. He used the rug to close it and tossed it away.

He got into the car, its motor still running, and drove around the long circular driveway to the narrow road that led to the river, then went along that road until he came to the large billboard he had fixed in his mind as a landmark. He turned there, drove until he reached the water tower, another landmark, and stayed on that road until he came to the home.

He turned off the lights as he drove up the driveway into the lot. He wasn't sure which spot it had been in, except that there were cars on both sides. He chose one that seemed close to it anyway, turned off the motor and slipped out, closing the door quietly. Anxious to get in, he decided to hold on to the car keys until tomorrow when he hid the gun. Now, staying within the shadows of the building, he walked around to the side and unlocked the door slowly, trying to prevent even the faintest click.

Across. Made it. He pulled off his clothes hurriedly and slipped into bed. He drew the blanket over him.

Josie, I'm home.

21

Captain Denny and LaSala were among the first detectives to converge on the house, for the call from the first officers to arrive there made it sound like a twin to the Leonard murders: a husband and wife, no apparent signs of ransacking.

They were the Dodmans, Lawrence and Carol; she was fifty-three, he was forty-nine. The maid, who had found the bodies that morning after letting herself in with her key, was sitting in the kitchen, racked with gasps. "They were so happy. Their daughter was married Saturday. Their only child. It was so beautiful. Everything was so beautiful."

Lawrence Dodman's older brother, their closest relative, had been summoned, was there with his two sons. He kept repeating that it made no sense, they had no enemies, it had to be a robber.

LaSala said, "What did he do?"

"What do you mean, what did he do?"

"His work."

"He had an interest in several companies, but he wasn't active in them."

"Is any of them a nursing home, a retirement home, a hospital?"

"Not that I know of."

"Was he involved with the aged in any way? By that I mean was he involved in a lawsuit, does he own property that caters to elderly people? Things like that."

"I can't think of anything. Maybe he was, but I don't know."

"What about Mrs. Dodman? Did she have any involvement with them? For instance, did she do any volunteer work in a home or hospital?"

"She may have, but again I don't know."

There was, if you averaged it out, about a homicide a day in the city. Most solved themselves: the wife was still holding the gun, or kid gang members shot each other on the street. Most of the others gave you at least a direction: the cash register was empty, the girl was raped. But this one belonged to the rest: you didn't know anything until eventually, if ever, you found out.

LaSala watched as they were carrying out the bodies, covered and strapped. The investigator from the medical examiner's office had said he was sure they had been dead since at least midnight. Since no one reported it, and the houses were so far apart, the odds were that none of the neighbors heard a thing. But the men canvassing the homes were still out.

You, he thought, looking at the panting dog, they should have sold.

He walked out to see how the search of the grounds was going. Newsmen, who were being kept outside, tried to get his attention. Two television cameras homed in on him. Someone held a microphone to his face. "No comment. Please."

A reporter from the *Sun-Journal,* whom he had known for years, said, "Nick, I want to talk to you."

"Pal, what can I say to you? We don't know anything. I really can't talk to you right now, Jer."

"But I have something to tell you. You know, they had this big wedding Saturday. It must have been a real wingding because it got quite a spread in the society section. You know I like to play detective. What I'm saying, it could have tipped off a thief."

"Could be." Did he really think they wouldn't think of that?

"Nick?" he said as LaSala started to walk off. "Remember the big play they got years ago? When they broke the old man's will?"

The captain slept fitfully, kept waking from dreams he couldn't remember. The one he finally woke from in the morning left him frightened, but he didn't know why. He calmed down, however, when he recalled that this wasn't unusual. Sometimes, maybe three times, this would happen in the morning after an execution.

Soon he was fine. The two of them were gone; he had helped make the world a little better again.

When he went for his clothes he remembered that he had to hide the stuff. He dressed carefully, making sure nothing dropped from his pockets.

He was walking out of the room when he saw the will he had left on the night table. He folded it and put it in his pocket. The Lord—and he was returning to the Lord—must have shaken his head, said to Himself, "Captain, I still need you there."

LaSala certainly did remember the case now, but it had happened so long ago that he had forgotten about it. He felt like a goof, but the others should too. The older ones, that is.

Even so, he didn't remember all the details and he went with Goldner to the *Sun-Journal* and had them bring out the old clippings.

Mrs. Dodman's father, Charles Rouse, had owned one of the largest radio stations in the city. He sold it several years before his death, which was almost sixteen years ago. Mrs. Dodman, his only child, had taken him to court, claiming that he was mentally incompetent and had fallen under the influence of a Dr. Stanford Wilkinson, chief of medicine at Hamley Memorial Hospital.

During the hearing Rouse, who was seventy-seven at the time, claimed that his daughter and son-in-law had hired a guard, pretending to be a servant, to hold him a prisoner in his home, while his daughter claimed that Dr. Wilkinson was draining money from him. Rouse died during the hearing, and it was then learned that he had changed his will a few years before, leaving a little under a million dollars to his daughter and over twenty million to charity, the bulk of it to set up a cancer research center at the hospital. But the daughter charged that the purpose of the center was actually to promote a drug that Dr. Wilkinson was working on but which the American Medical Association said was worthless. The will was ruled invalid and she got the entire estate.

What could this have to do with a series of murders sixteen years later?

Don't go nuts giving it too much thought, LaSala cautioned himself. First hear from Ballistics.

It was strange, the captain thought, how sometimes he couldn't remember something that happened that morning, but events of years ago could come back in every detail. And so it was when he had seen the pictures of them standing near their pool and dancing together with huge smiles. It wasn't their faces that brought the thunder to his head; he didn't remember their faces; but the name. He could still hear the way Charlie Rouse used to say it. He never called his son-in-law by his first name. Disliked him too much. It was always Dodman.

Charlie used to like to go out with him on some of his raids. He would use the excuse that he was covering them for the station, and maybe that was part of it, but he was really a nut on policework and crime. The last member of a family that owned a large department store, he had often told him how he had always been interested in show business, had even gone into vaudeville as a young man. In a way, he had stayed in show business by buying the radio station instead of taking over the store.

A real charitable guy. A good guy.

And the daughter gave him nothing but trouble.

"Hughie," Charlie once said to him, "she's up to her third now." After that divorce: "It's four now. Dodman. King of the leeches." Then a couple of years before the end: "They're out to murder me, Hughie." And though the captain didn't really believe it, this was *Charlie,* so he had a couple men watch him day and night for a while.

They did kill him. Taking him to court killed him. Not only had they killed him and broken his will and destroyed his name, they even moved into his home afterward. So it was only justice that the law should at last close in on them there.

Only one of the slugs was in good enough shape to be tested and compared. And when word came through that it was from the same gun, the immediate dilemma was whether the motive was rooted in something relatively recent or in that old incident.

Dr. Wilkinson, they had already learned, had died five years ago, leaving no immediate family. One of the possibilities was that a friend or colleague had been clutching this old grudge for sixteen years. Yet if that was so, they wondered, why had he killed the nurse and Mr. and Mrs. Leonard? And why kill them first?

"We're talking as if this guy's a perfectly normal, logical person," Inspector McDowell said, meeting with Denny and LaSala. "He may have forgotten all about the Dodmans. So if they really were killed because of that whole business—and I can't think of a much bigger if—maybe someone recently reminded him about it. Or maybe the story on the wedding did it."

Back at his desk, LaSala thought of Rouse. He remembered him from two raids, once wearing a coat over his pajamas because the captain had let him know in the dead of night and he had come straight from bed.

Funny. Latimore from the nursing home. Rouse from his past.

Jesus, he thought. Captain, you're right in the middle and you can't help us one bit.

22

Dr. Andrew Goldstein, who had been associated with Dr. Wilkinson at Hamley Memorial and was now emeritus professor of medicine at University Hospital, gave long thought to LaSala's question. "No, I can't think of anyone. I think everyone who knew Dr. Wilkinson, really knew him, was very upset about what happened. But to carry a grudge all these years? No, I can't think of anyone. You know, he really got a bad deal out of that. Now, he was doing research on Baeline—that's the name they gave it—and it didn't work out, but that wasn't the only drug he was working on. The daughter made it sound as if that was the one and only thing he was interested in. Dr. Wilkinson did have his enemies in the profession, of course. But he was an extremely sound researcher and clinician. And I do know that after Mr. Rouse's will was broken, he was contemplating slander charges against the daughter and her husband, but I really don't know what happened."

"Do you have any idea how he became involved with Rouse?"

"Yes. Dr. Wilkinson told me. Rouse had cancer phobia. His father and, I think, a grandfather had cancer and, in his later years in particular, that was very much on his mind. He came to see Dr.

Wilkinson because of his reputation, and Wilkinson assured him he didn't have cancer. But if you've ever met anyone with a phobia, you know it doesn't go away that easily. He saw Dr. Wilkinson rather frequently. Now he was extremely interested in the work Dr. Wilkinson was doing on Baeline, but I know for a fact that Dr. Wilkinson told him it was extremely experimental. So, the endowment was not just for research on that one drug. It was for cancer research in general. But her lawyer really destroyed him at the hearing—just kept hammering at Baeline and the 'terrible' influence he had on Rouse. Now the situation as I remember it was this. Two doctors said Rouse was mentally competent, two said he wasn't. And then when he died and the will came out, I guess the judge saw all the money as going to Baeline. But, as I say, I'm just guessing."

LaSala took a piece of paper from his pocket. He had written down the names of the four house doctors as well as a few other doctors who had been treating patients at the nursing home at the time of Latimore's murder. "Do you recognize any of these names? Would you remember if any of them were connected with Dr. Wilkinson?"

It was an extremely fragile hope: that this might be the link between the nursing home and the Dodmans. And it remained just that. Dr. Goldstein couldn't connect any of the names.

The next day, while some of his men went to question the other doctors, LaSala stopped off briefly at the clinic to speak to David. But David, who had heard of Dr. Wilkinson, was easily able to assure him he had never met him.

"By the way, Doc," LaSala said, "are they ever going to find something that clears up senility? I'm thinking of one of your patients. Poor Captain Hughes. I used to work for him, you know."

"Really?"

"Quite a few years. He was some cop."

"Well, he's nowhere as bad as a lot of them there. In fact, I wouldn't really call him senile. He might have some memory lapses, and he has been losing ground lately, but he can be strong as a bull, give you hell."

"I've seen him, could hardly move. I think he just about said my name. And once, right in front of me, pissed himself."

"The captain? That's unusual. He's not incontinent."

Who, LaSala said to himself when he was leaving, is that guy treating? Maybe you get so used to that scene, even the captain seems pretty good.

He was sitting in the lounge, arms folded, and staring at the floor, when someone said hello. He looked up and saw a woman smiling at him, carmel-colored hands clutched at her waist. For a moment he thought she was an Indian.

"I'm Mary Lions. Mary Darling Lions. I don't usually talk to gentlemen first but you look very nice. My husband was the Reverend Lions. He's dead, poor thing. He was pastor of the Church of the Sacred Zion and the congregation has been very nice to me, they are helping pay for me here, though I do have Social Security, God bless Franklin Delano Roosevelt. He was the president who passed it, you know. Does one just go about introducing one's self? Nobody introduces you."

He shrugged, feeling obliged to do something.

"Were you operated on?" she asked. "Oh, that operation. Do you know I was on the table eight hours and three hours in the recovery room. Belle told me that. You see, she and George were waiting. They were so worried. Cancer isn't very serious any more, you know. They know how to treat it. Do they let you take baths whenever you want here? I like a bath in the morning and a bath at night."

Good-o, he thought.

She stood there still smiling, still clutching those hands. Then she glanced about, smiling at everything, as though waiting for someone to ask her to dance.

"It was very nice chatting with you," she said.

She walked off. Later, when he glanced over briefly, he saw her standing and talking to a toothless woman who kept hitting at her tray, and afterward saw her standing by Sporty as he sat next to the window.

It was Talk-Talk, the next day, who brought what was happening to his attention. "The bow tie's got himself a chocolate-covered girl friend."

He saw her, now, sitting with him by the window.

"Maybe they'll give 'em a wedding," Talk-Talk said. "Captain, ask me nice I'll dance with you."

And the day after that they sat on the sofa next to him, holding hands.

"You're so fortunate to have a daughter, Mr. Heggens. My husband and I were childless, you see. As the Bible says, I am barren. But we had a fine marriage. You simply shouldn't expect her to visit you often. Children have to live their own lives."

"She is a real thoroughbred. I hope you will have the pleasure of meeting her shortly. And my grandchild. And my son-in-law. A fine fellow. Rides too. My daughter's the champion, though. I told you we manufacture golf balls."

"Do you like ice cream, Mr. Heggens?"

The captain got up and walked away. Black and white was fine, but no holding hands. He didn't have to sit there and watch that. Yet a little later that day, when Reds called, "Mary, can I see you dear?" but motioned for Sporty to stay where he was, he felt flame at what she was up to. But he didn't say anything until she called to Mary again when she went back to him.

"Whyn't you leave 'em alone. Ain't hurting you."

"What're you talking about?"

"You know what I'm talking about. Let 'em alone."

"Captain, will you get out of my hair?"

But he noticed with great satisfaction that she didn't call to Mary again.

Back in his room he sat in the chair and stared out the window. He thought of Charlie Rouse. He recalled Charlie suggesting that he grab early pension and come work for him. "I'm a cop, Charlie. I'm no good at 'This is QDLQ.' They'd run you off the air." And Charlie laughing, "I don't mean that, Hughie. You got a good head, I can use you." "I'm a cop, Charlie."

Charlie a millionaire and him a cop, but good friends, real good friends. And no one took a friend of his and yelled out to the whole world he was crazy and then jumped on his grave and grabbed his dough.

23

Pat took the couple into the office behind the nursing station, where the husband, a man in his mid-forties, slumped into a chair and began sobbing. Then, rubbing a hand at his face, he said, "I don't know how to leave her. Jesus, this is hard. How do you just go out and leave her? How do you leave your mother? She had a beautiful home, Pop was a great guy—God, if he saw her now—she loved her kids."

"Yeah, and look which one is here," his wife said. "Sal. Everything on Sal. Where's Tony? Where's Pauline? You're here, they're not here."

"Pauline's sick, you know Pauline's sick. Tony, he's got to work. Don't talk that way. I don't want you to talk that way. They love her, they'd do anything for her. Christ, I feel lousy," he said, wiping at his eyes. "Miss, tell me. Honest to God, tell me. We doing the right thing?"

"Your mother needs someone to be with her twenty-four hours a day, Mr. Coletti. Now if you can't give that kind of care you can't give it. So, yes, you're doing the right thing."

"It's not like you're dumping her, Sal," his wife said. "The Mazettos, they really dumped the old lady. She was as clear as me. But this is an old, old woman, she can't walk, she don't know who you are, someone's got to feed her, she got no control. It's a terrible thing you get old you got no control."

"She was a real lady," he said to Pat. "You should have seen her just two years ago. Our daughter's wedding. She *danced.* Wasn't the same woman. *Danced.* And she always held herself like this." He held his head, his arms a certain way. "Like she was a queen. Marie, isn't that what people always used to say? She holds herself like a queen. Real dignity. . . . So, you really mean it? We're doing the right thing?"

"I really mean it. We'll give her everything she needs. And you can visit at any time and call us at any time to see how she is."

He stood up. Suddenly there was a little smile. "You like tomatoes? I'm in the produce business. Tomatoes right now are great. I'm gonna get you a big box."

"You just go about your day. We're here to take care of her. So try to relax. And remember, she's in good hands."

"You're really great. You don't know what you lifted from my heart."

After they left, she went in to see the new patient again. Terry and a new aide were trying to get her into a wheelchair. "Who are you?" she was saying to Terry.

"I'm Terry Dougherty. Say Ter-ry."

"No you ain't! You ain't Mike! Mike!" she called. "Mike!"

Pat helped them with her, then went back to the station and left word with Dr. Kliegman's service for him to call the home: since they went by turn, this would be his patient. A nurse from Wing C came up to her.

"Just to let you know, the story's absolutely not true."

"Are you sure?"

"It wasn't in the papers, so the office called one of them and asked. It never happened."

Pat shook her head. When they had come in this morning an aide from the night shift said she had heard over the radio that a nurse from a nearby nursing home had been murdered while walking to her car. "Is she crazy?" Pat said. "She must have heard something."

"I think every time she farts it goes right to her brain. Christ, I'm a nervous wreck."

Pat was still shaken too. But as she calmed down she tried to remember everything she had said to the Colettis, wasn't sure if she had given them enough time, had said all the things they wanted to hear. The latest murders were frightening enough without rumors; she was conscious enough that she was sitting in a murdered woman's chair.

He saw the door open as he pulled up the drive. He kissed her on the lips, then bent down and roughed it up with the dogs. "They don't bark at me any more," he said. "Good sign or bad?"

"Bad."

"I forgot the wine," he said, standing up.

"I forgot the dinner."

He sniffed the air. "Hey, that smells good."

"You wait in the living room till I finish. I don't like people watching me. There's Scotch in that closet."

He poured himself a short drink, put in ice, some water. "I can't watch?"

"Nope."

He went into the living room, kicked off his shoes and picked up a newspaper. The murders. He tossed it aside, thinking of Laura. The only time she'd ever said anything about any of them was after Kay was killed, when it seemed to be an isolated case. Not a word since the others. That was typical Laura: shut out anything that could conceivably cause her a shred of worry. Not that he was the slightest bit worried, but with him being in this field wasn't it at least something to mention?

He reached for a magazine. "Do you like reading *Playboy*?"

"Not really. I'm looking for my picture."

"How much would it take for you to pose?"

"Oh, do they pay money?"

"Hey, you're funny. I thought you said you weren't funny."

"Dinner."

She had roasted a duck, which was not crisp enough for him, though he made all the appropriate comments and sounds. Afterward she made Irish coffee. "Let's take it outside," she said.

They sat on the open porch. It was black out, the air punctuated with the sound of crickets.

"Hey, you know your patient Mr. Heggens?"

"Of course I know my patient Mr. Heggens. The kid with all that acne."

"Seriously," she laughed. "Have you seen him lately?"

"About two weeks ago, I think."

"Well, you should see him since. He has a lady friend. A beautiful black woman. Brown woman. You should see them. They're always hand in hand. The beautiful part is he's not moping any more, sitting at the window waiting for his daughter. He looks as proud as a penguin. In fact, we had a little time of it yesterday. They were missing. They turned up in the tool shed."

"They thought it was the movies?"

"You are terrible, you know that? They were sitting there holding hands. I'm afraid we got to the scene too soon."

"You think they went there to . . . uh . . . make out?"

"I don't understand what you mean, sir. Do you mean to screw?"

"That's the expression," he said, snapping his fingers. "Do you think they went there to screw?"

"I would certainly hope so. Cummings had a bird. He yelled at them like they were ten years old."

"Would you want anyone doing it on your tools?"

"Oh Jesus," she laughed and reached over and took his hand. They stood up and he brought her to him and kissed her cheek, then her mouth. She squeezed him hard, then her arms fell away and her hand found his again. "Let's take a walk."

"To the tool shed, I trust."

They walked out on the grounds. "We used to have a stream running through here but it dried up."

"How long have you lived here?"

"I think—let's see, eleven years. My husband's parents bought this for us when we got married—bought him everything. They didn't do him a favor."

"Has he remarried?"

"I don't know."

"Can I ask the question?"

"The question? What's the question?"

"How can someone like you still be at large?"

"Very easy. It can get mighty cold out there, sir. Not that I haven't been asked. But I seem to attract creatures from outer space. Be prepared for a UFO."

"What do you do for fun?"

"Oh . . . play tennis, I have girl friends, I date now and then, I like to swim, water ski, I like to read. I've sailed, but I'm not very good."

"Hey, is this a fence?"

"It's a fence. Would you like to meet the Brainards?"

"No, I wouldn't like to meet the Brainards."

They were walking back now.

"Tell me about you," she said.

"Oh . . . I'm sure you've seen the movie."

She squeezed his hand and he stopped. He put his arms around her and kissed her on the forehead, then her lips, softly at first, gently, then hard. Then he just held onto her, not sure if it was his heart he was hearing or both of theirs.

That Sunday the captain was in the front lounge when Sporty's daughter came in. When he saw her stop just inside the doorway, mouth open and eyes wide, he couldn't imagine what was wrong. He looked over his shoulder to see what she was staring at.

He was so used to the sight that he wondered why it should startle her to see them walking toward her holding hands.

A couple days later he woke up sick to the stomach and feverish. When he didn't go for breakfast, Garbo came in. "Is something wrong, Captain?"

"Don't know."

She came over and felt his forehead. Then she shook down a thermometer and inserted it in his mouth. When she read it she told him he had a little over a hundred, that it was nothing to be concerned about, but to stay in bed.

He felt so weak he didn't protest and fell back to sleep. The sound of crying woke him, then a woman's voice: "Now what did I do? Why are you doing this?"

He got up and went to the doorway. Two uniformed ambulance attendants, one of them holding a suitcase, were leading Mary toward the door at the end of the hall.

"Why? I insist why?" she cried.

Suddenly Sporty was out of his room. "What's going on? What's going on? Where are you taking her?"

The door opened and closed on them firmly.

The captain stood staring at the door. He looked over at the station. Garbo and one of the aides were talking to each other and crying. He stared at the door again.

The daughter . . . it had to be that goddamn daughter!

24

That afternoon he opened his eyes with great effort to see Dr. Benny standing by his bed.

"Sorry I had to wake you, Captain, but I hear you don't feel well. Would you open your pajama top for me?"

He took deep breaths and then short, according to instructions as the stethoscope was moved about his chest, and he turned to one side as Dr. Benny tapped his back and then probed around some more. He opened his mouth for the tongue depressor and light, then turned his head to each side as the doctor looked into his ears. He lowered his pajama bottoms now. No, this didn't hurt, nor that, nor that.

Dr. Benny was doing some monkeyshines with his feet, running some kind of instrument along the soles; asked him did he feel anything on his toes and he said yes, sort of a sticking, and now the doctor was bending his knees and feeling his calves.

"Look, I want to check your prostate. Would you lie on your side?" And he lay on his side, not liking this one bit, but too weak, too drained and feverish to complain.

"There," Dr. Benny said, rising. "That's fine. I'm sure the only thing wrong is a little bug, and we'll give you something for that. Other than some aches and pains, is everything O.K.?"

He was writing something on a pad now, intent on just that; and the captain, meanwhile, wanted to say something like he hated being here, and he was mad, he was mad at his kids and Sporty's kid and everyone's kids, and he felt so fucken blue and tired and he was scared of dying and scared of losing all his memory. Looking up, Dr. Benny said, reaching over and touching him, "Look, you're going to be fine. You'll have to be in bed a few days, maybe three, maybe five. So just take it easy."

He was walking off now. "Hey, young fellow," he said to No Voice. Then he was out in the hall.

The captain stared after him, too tired to be real angry and yet thinking, even as he started closing his eyes: Why the fuck did you bother to ask?

Pat handed him the captain's chart at the station and he riffled through the papers, saying, "It's not pneumonia, that was my concern. I think he had this before. Yeah," he said stopping at a page. "I see he didn't have any problems with tetracycline. So we'll start him on that."

"I want you to see Mr. Heggens. I'm more worried about him than the captain. It's terrible. I only learned this morning what they were going to do; they never told me. I called you, you weren't in. I thought maybe you could stop it."

"I'm sorry. I called as soon as I got your message. Now tell me again just what happened. And try to calm down. You were a mess on the phone."

"I'm still a mess. I'm so goddamn mad. Look at this." She held out a hand. It was trembling.

"Now calm down. Will you try to calm down?"

"I came in this morning and there's this official note, 'Director of Nurses' and all that, that we're to pack Mary Lions, she's leaving. Ordinarily I wouldn't question it, but this is too fast. It doesn't generally happen this fast. You get some kind of notice. I went to the office and asked Doral what it's all about, and all she says is that we're supposed to pack her. But she motions me to go out in the hall. She told me that Heggens' daughter was in Sunday and saw them holding hands and went into the office and raised all kinds of hell. She put it to them: get rid of Mary or she was pulling out her father. So, they got rid of Mary. After all, her money might run out. His, never."

"Where is she?"

"I don't know. You know, her church was largely supporting her here. They told the minister some kind of story, she wasn't working out, I don't know. Maybe she's at another home. Maybe a private home. I just don't know. But it was terrible. She was crying, Mr. Heggens was crying, I'm crying, Terry's crying. And he's back at the window again."

David went into the room. Heggens didn't seem to know he was there, just kept staring out. David said, "Mr. Heggens?" When he finally looked around, "I stopped in to say hello to you."

Heggens nodded slightly. He still had on the jacket with leather elbows, but the top few buttons of his shirt were open, his bow tie dangling down one side of his collar.

David kneeled in front of his chair. "Let's see a smile there," he said. "I don't want you to just sit here. It's not good for you. Come on, look at me, I want to talk to you," for he was starting to look away again. "Hey, everyone loves you, you know that? Your daughter. Everyone here. Everyone's worried about you."

He got no response. Not knowing what else to do, he took his pulse, simply to hold his arm for a while. "Very good." He stood up. "Does anything hurt you?"

Mr. Heggens shook his head without looking at him.

"I'm going to give you something," he said. "I don't want you just sitting here. Will you promise me you'll try to snap out of it?" Nothing. No nod, no shake of the head. Feeling helpless, he walked out to the hall. Pat was waiting. He went with her to the station. "I want him outside, even if you have to pick him up and carry him. Has he been involved in any activities?"

"We've never been able to get him interested. The only thing that worked was Mary. He became a different person."

"Let me see his chart." Going through it he said, "We can up his Elavil a little, but I don't want to go too high." He took out his pen, clicked it open.

"Let's go in there," she said softly, nodding toward the little office. Sitting across from him she said, "Antidepressants, outside, recreation, picnics—they're not going to work. They didn't work before and they're not going to work now. He's a heartbroken guy. If that son of a bitch of a daughter would show up at least once a week maybe he'd have a chance. Maybe every three weeks she shows up, and she doesn't want him holding hands. I'd like to kick her right in the, excuse the expression, right in the cunt."

"Being black didn't help. But my guess is it could have been any woman."

"You live to seventy, eighty and you've got to ask your goddamn kids' permission to screw! I could just kill myself that I didn't guess this might happen. I should have tried to see to it they weren't together on Sundays."

"So, the daughter would show up on a Monday."

"I guess you're right. Do you know what burns me up? Really burns me up? If she wanted to move her father, let her move her father. That's bad enough, but if that's what she wants that's what she wants. But don't do that to someone else. Poor Mary. You know what's going to happen at the next place? She's going to carry the label that she was too much to handle here. Do you know how many strikes that starts you off with?"

"It's a bitch."

"And that poor guy in there. David, call the daughter."

"And say what?"

"Tell her what's already happening to her father. I would do it myself but it won't carry the same weight. Tell her to come in every week or get Mrs. Lions back."

"Wait a minute, wait a minute. Whoa there. You've told her not to keep telling him she's coming back tomorrow, and I've discussed it with her. But it didn't do any good and it's not *going* to do any good. She's not going to come in any more than she wants to or can, and she's going to say whatever she wants. If we couldn't change her before, we're not going to change her now. I'll call her, of course, but it's just going to be another call. Now, as for her asking them to bring Mrs. Lions back, you know there isn't one chance in hell of that."

"Then talk to the office."

"Pat, they're not going to bring her back. You're being irrational."

"Well, at least I'm being *something*."

"What the hell is that supposed to mean?"

"I don't know. I just don't want them to get away with this. David, Heggens is *your* patient. They had no right to do anything to your patient without letting you know."

"Pat," he said as though talking to a child, "they didn't do anything to my patient."

"Are you kidding? You must be kidding."

"Will you wait? Will you just let me finish? They didn't do anything to my patient, they didn't go against any of my orders. They didn't change medicines, they didn't put him in restraints. What they did was throw someone else out. I don't like it any more than you. But this is a matter of dollars and cents to them. This is a business. I go in there, what do I say? 'I want Mrs. Lions back.' 'Well, *we* don't want Mrs. Lions back.' 'If you don't get her back I quit.' Is that what you want?"

"No. I just want you to tell them how you feel."

"I should go in there and say, 'I don't like what you did to Mrs. Lions.' They say, 'Well, that's nice. So what else is new?' I'm not going to start something I can't do anything about, and I'm not about to have a fight I can't win. Listen, I've had one heart attack, I really don't need another."

She glared at him. Then she whirled and went out to the station, picked something up from the counter and stared at it.

Standing next to her, he said, "Can we be a little reasonable?"

She didn't answer.

He felt a surge of anger that she was doing this to him, was so goddamn stubborn, was making him feel as though he had failed a test.

"Can we talk?"

She didn't look up.

He walked away. She'd calm down. If not, maybe just as well. He liked her . . . loved her—but this was a new face, this was a loony.

She got out of the car and, as usual, bent down as the dogs leaped up at her. It made her feel better for a while. She went into the house and poured a little Scotch into a tall glass, filled it with ice and water, then sat out on the porch.

She had held herself in until the end of her shift, then had gone into the office. Though she had promised herself this wouldn't happen, it had ended in a fight. And with her without a job, as of *now.*

She wondered what he would do when he heard about it. Call her? What would she say if he did?

If he called right now, it would be no. Or even next year, the way she felt. Not that he would have accomplished anything more, but that didn't really matter: she had wanted him simply to speak out, to say this was wrong, to put his feelings on the line. To be as special as she'd come to think he was.

Pat, for Christ's sake, you deserve someone special.

She felt her eyes start to fill, then brushed at them and smiled as though amused by her own assessment of herself.

Well, you do deserve someone special.

Goddamn it, none of that smile, *you do.*

She took a sip from her glass as though to drink to that. Then she went inside to look at a curtain in the kitchen which needed sewing or a new one. Sewing, she decided, might do it. She didn't mind being out of a job for a while, she thought. Sleep late. Relax. Get her head together. Go to a resort with Helen, do some water skiing. Then, in a couple of weeks, get another job.

Maybe this time, though, she would go into pediatrics.

No, she wouldn't. She knew herself too well. She had quit geriatric nursing once, only to feel guilty about it and return in a month. Even now, thinking of the patients at Linwood, she felt as if she had abandoned them.

Though she wouldn't go back there, in a few weeks at most she would be at another home.

25

Since they were coming up with nothing else that seemed to tie the Dodman murders to the "geriatric killings," as one newspaper began calling them, the police were now giving considerably more weight to the possibility that the motive was somehow linked to the breaking of the will. Detective Goldner spent two days going through the records of the proceedings, only to report to LaSala that he didn't find anything that looked important.

"There's something sort of interesting though," Goldner said. "Did you know that Captain Hughes had Rouse guarded for a while?"

"No."

"I thought you might since you were on his squad."

"When was it? It might have been before my time."

"A couple years before Rouse died."

"No, that would have been after my time. I think I was on Major Thefts then. What was it about?"

"He was afraid his daughter would murder him."

"The captain thought that?"

"No, that came out wrong. Rouse was afraid his daughter was going to murder him. And the captain put a couple men on him. The judge really gave it to him for that. He could have been in a mess."

"Let's back up. What was the captain doing at the hearing?"

"This was after Rouse died. The Dodmans apparently subpoenaed him as their witness, to prove Rouse was off his head, but you can tell the captain wasn't happy about that. After he said he was guarding him against his daughter, the judge wanted to know how long this went on and he said about a week. And the judge said something like, 'Was any attempt made on his life?' The captain said no. 'Did you think his life was really in danger?' 'No.' 'Then, why did you guard him?' 'He was an old man and I didn't want him scared.' 'Did you think he was mentally incompetent?' 'No.' The judge then wanted to know was it his practice to spend city money guarding people he didn't think were in danger, did the commissioner know about it, things like that. Then you can see the captain pulling out of it. 'I didn't think he was in danger but I couldn't be sure. I don't go bothering the commissioner with every little thing.' He was really great."

"That sounds typical. He was one of a kind. Christ, I'm talking like he's dead. But I guess that's the way I think of him these days."

Still thinking about the captain after Goldner left, he found himself smiling at the memory of a few similar incidents. That was him all right: if you were his friend, you truly had a friend. He could bend a rule or three if you were his friend or it meant breaking a case.

For the first time in a long while he thought about the pack of cigarettes in the bottom drawer of his desk. He had given up smoking a few years ago but always kept a pack there "in case." The most he had ever done was put an unlighted one in his lips, and he hadn't done even that in about a year. But he had one there now.

Funny how the captain was the only person they knew about who, though only so vaguely, popped up in two of the cases.

He pulled in on the cigarette, then looked at it and threw it into his wastepaper basket. He sat back in his swivel chair, thinking. This was crazy, but who knew? After all, the killings themselves were . . . crazy.

What if someone who was real close to the captain thought that his nurse had mistreated him? All right—but why the Leonards? Maybe the Leonards because it spread into a hatred against anyone who did anything against the aged; that, or he wanted to draw attention away from the nursing home. Then, after reading about the wedding, he remembered what the Dodmans did to the captain's old friend.

But who? Who was that close?

Could he possibly get the captain to remember if he had ever complained to anyone about Kay Latimore? If so, if he could manage just that, it could be a beginning.

Although he doubted if he would accomplish anything, he drove to the nursing home. There he learned that the captain had been sick for the past few days and that, though he was still in bed, was feeling much better.

"Is it all right if I talk to him?"

"You can certainly try."

He walked into his room. The captain, lying against two pillows, seemed to be looking past him as he came in. LaSala sat next to him. "Captain, it's me again, Nick LaSala. Your old squad?" He wasn't sure if there was any recognition. "Remember your nurse, Mrs. Latimore? Kay Latimore?"

"La-Sal?"

"Right. Right. Nick LaSala. Captain, try to remember something for me. Do you remember Kay Latimore? Mrs. Latimore? Your nurse?"

"More?"

Not long afterward LaSala was walking slowly back to his car. You really had to be desperate to try that route.

So, who was that close to him?

The closest one he could think of, certainly the one to begin with, was the son.

He lay there after LaSala left, almost completely calm. But LaSala had made him think of her again; it all came back, her walking into the room and seeing Missy, her threats, his pleading, her going ahead with it with Dr. Benny.

"I put her in the goddamn chair for you, Missy."

He was suddenly aware he had said that out loud. What else had he said?

He turned toward the other bed, a quick stabbing in his chest. No Voice was staring at him. What made it even more frightening was that he quickly looked away.

He thought: I've got to kill him.

All he had to do was creep out of bed tonight, put a pillow on his face and just press down.

Immediately he shook it from his thoughts. *He,* a captain of detectives, contemplating murder?

He was in bed only five days, but when he came out of the room for the first time it was as though passing through a veil into a strange world. The first three days were a jumble in his mind of shitting in a pan and pissing in a bottle and swallowing stuff he didn't like, and some new broad on the morning shift, all blonde curls and smiles, saying Walt this and Walt that. He hadn't been called Walt since he was a kid, and he didn't like it. Even Josie, God rest her soul, called him Hughie when she wasn't calling him Daddy.

The past two days he had been able to work his way over to the bathroom in his room. But that had been his world, those walls, that bathroom, a few faces, that fucken Walt shit, and glimpses into the open doorway of the room across the hall.

He still felt weak, fuzzy; didn't have strength as yet to get out of his pajamas and robe. He had had breakfast in bed, and now, reaching for the railing along the wall out there, he stepped into the hall. Here and there were people in wheelchairs, but either he had forgotten most of their faces or most were new. Talk-Talk was still there, however, though the captain had forgotten how much like a parakeet he looked. That dumb stupid baseball cap! Why do you let 'em do that to you?

"Welcome! Welcome to the land of depression! Did you see me looking in? I would have come in, but I don't need a bug. Depressed enough without a bug. Young docs never get a bug. I never got a bug from a patient in my life."

"It's good to see you out here, Walt," she said from the station. "How do you feel?"

"Walt?" Talk-Talk said, looking at her. "That's the captain, lady. Highest ranking officer in the house. Respect!" But she was opening up a file cabinet. "That's another one," he said to the captain. "Talking to her's like talking to a wall. Our pretty lady was canned. I heard them talking—they won't say why. Hey, blondie, why was she canned?"

"Why was *who* canned?"

"Don't give me that. I got ears. Hey!" He whistled to get her attention. But though she walked toward him it was only to pass by. She tapped him on the shoulders. "Doc, be a good boy."

"Boy my ass! You couldn't work two minutes for me!"

It was strange not seeing Garbo there. It made him feel uneasy. It was something like the feeling he used to have each time he was moved: what had gone wrong?

Had she killed someone? Been caught screwing Benny?

He felt dizzy all at once. Without realizing it, he had gone farther down the hall than he thought. He held onto the railing, eased himself into a chair. Talk-Talk wheeled himself over.

"Do you talk?" he said.

"No. I'm a chimpanzee."

"You never talk."

He was surprised. He talked so much in his head he felt he talked too much.

"Tell me how many enemas they gave you."

"Don't know."

"They're big on enemas. They think the answer to everything is shitting. Captain, I got to talk to someone. I'm a pain in the ass, but I'm down. This time I'm really down. I feel like going skiddoo. If I had enough pills I'd go skiddoo today. You know how my wife died? A bee bit her. A little bee and she blew up and died. Raised the kids myself. Christ, where's the bee? I need that bee."

As he sat there his head began drooping. But he looked up soon, as though waking suddenly. His voice sounded tired now.

"You know? I really wasn't just an asshole doctor. I feel so shitty I made it up. I did hemorrhoids, but I did a lot of other things too. Took out tonsils, adenoids, appendixes. I took out one tumor bigger than my head. I took out kidneys. You know, I only took out ten good appendixes in my whole life? Nine. I should claim a record. You know what my ambition was? To operate on the president of the United States. Save his life, and it would be in the papers, and me and Hannah would be at the White House all the time. Next to that I wanted to operate on a movie star. Used to dream I'd get a call, come out here, you're the only one can save her. Or him. Someone with a big name. Go to previews with them."

His head was drooping again. Though his eyes were slightly open, he seemed asleep. The captain stood up. Heading back he happened to glance into a room and saw a figure by a window, tied in a chair and rocking back and forth against the restraints. The face looked familiar. Then he saw it was Sporty. He couldn't believe that cavernous face was Sporty.

He wondered where what's her name . . . Mary, where Mary was. Then he remembered what happened to Mary.

"Captain, something wrong?" An aide took his arm.

"Want to go back the room."

"Sure."

He didn't want to be helped but he needed it. He got back in bed. He felt a heaviness on his head, his chest, as though the air itself were pressing against him. He hated this place, but it was all that was left and it seemed to be falling apart, too. He lay there until someone came in and asked was he going to have lunch in the room. He wanted to, but somehow he knew that the only way he was going to get his strength back, be captain again, was to start using his legs more. He looked at his legs, bright white, muscular, here and there knotted with varicose veins, and willed strength into them and got out of bed and made his way to the dining room.

On the way back, he stopped by Sporty's room again. Still rocking.

"Hey," the captain said.

He didn't look over; kept rocking.

The following day he saw the albino and another orderly pushing a bed down the hall, one of those with blankets and filled plastic bags lying on a sheet that seemed to be covering pillows. He had seen plenty go by, generally not feeling much about it, but this one brought a clutching to his heart and he followed it down the hall. He saw the albino take out a key and open the door, holding it open with his hip until he and the other orderly began working the bed through. The captain took several long shaky strides, got to the door before it swung all the way closed. They whirled as he entered.

"Captain, you ain't allowed in here."

He grabbed hold of the sheet and pulled, scattering some of the blankets and bundles to the floor. He thought it might be Talk-Talk or Sporty, but it was a woman, skeletal except for her lips and cheeks which seemed stuffed with cotton.

He didn't recall ever seeing her. Even so, he kicked at one of the bundles as he walked out.

Dear God, make him strong again.

Dear God, let all of them lie like that some day.

26

During the week before her murder Kay Latimore had made only one reference to the captain in her notes, other than about such things as his medication and how he was eating and sleeping. It was something the police had seen early in the investigation and it seemed as innocuous now as it did then. She had written simply that he had "acted up" when he learned that a Mrs. VanEllen had to be sent to a mental hospital.

LaSala was hoping he would come up with something more than that when he spoke to the son. But Mark didn't even know what that referred to.

"I have no idea at all," he said, sitting across from LaSala in his den. "I guess it means what it says—he got upset. Did you see him when you were there? Then you know the shape he's in. It doesn't take much to get him upset. He's cranky, he's irritable, he's a totally different person. That's what old age has done to him. It kills us thinking of him in a nursing home, but there was nothing else we could do."

"I tell you, I got the shock of my life when I saw him."

"I tell myself it's not really my father. I mean it's him but it's not really him there. I don't know if you know what I mean. Anyway, we want him to be as comfortable as possible, to be free of pain, to have as peaceful an end as possible. They tell us he's strong, he can linger on for years."

"Let me ask you something else about Mrs. Latimore. Try not to take this wrong, but I've really got to ask. Did you have any feelings one way or the other about how she was treating your father?"

"I'll answer that, but wait a second," he said, annoyed. "I must be a little thick because it's only now starting to hit me. Do you think," and he smiled and touched his chest, "I killed her? I'm the guy?"

"No I don't. But the truth is, and I'll just tell you straight, I really don't know. I've got to do this. Look, your father was my boss. He taught me almost everything I know about being a cop. Now let's say he was on this case. He'd kick my butt if I didn't talk to you, I didn't talk to everyone I had some questions to ask."

He nodded. "I'm sorry. I really am. The fact is, I hardly knew her. My sisters, I'm sure, hardly knew her. About the only time we visit is Sunday, when I think she was on maybe twice."

"I haven't told you yet, but the reason I'm here is not only because of the nurse but because your father also knew the Dodmans, the couple who were murdered. It's complicated and I won't go into it, but actually he was a good friend of Mrs. Dodman's father. Charles Rouse. Do you remember your dad ever talking about Rouse?"

Mark frowned as he thought. "It doesn't ring a bell. And if it had anything to do with his work he probably never mentioned him at home. He rarely if ever talked about his work."

"Do many of your relatives or your father's friends visit him much at the home?"

"There's my sisters of course. There's an uncle, an aunt, but I don't know when's the last time they were there. Friends? I don't know. My father hasn't had very many friends these past few years. Oh, there's one I know about who visits him occasionally. Yorky. John Yorky. Fact is, you probably know him. Dad grabbed him. He busted out of prison a few times."

"This an ex-con?" He looked startled.

"That's right."

"An ex-*con*?"

When he saw that it wasn't Talk-Talk's body he stopped being concerned about him. It was as though he had been the victim of a joke, though by the beginning of the following week he began to worry about him again. Because Talk-Talk had stopped talking for longer than ever before. The staff seemed relieved about it, even joked about it, but it kept clinging to the captain's mind, digging in like something that had claws.

Talk-Talk was staying mostly in his room. They made him get into his wheelchair, insisted that he take his meals in the dining room, but he would wheel himself back immediately afterward. Occasionally, they would wheel him outside or into the hall or to one of the lounges and lock the chair in place. Sometimes he was able to reach down and unlock it; when he couldn't, he would just sit there staring. He refused to dress except for a robe over his pajamas.

At times they would try to kid him out of it. Doc, let's see a smile. Cat got your tongue? Tell us how you used to give the scrub nurses hell. Doc's in love.

Sometimes the captain would hear them discussing Doc. Most of them seemed to think it was just a phase. Some used the word "sour"; he was going sour, losing the will to live, that's what happens to a lot of 'em before they go.

The captain wasn't aware that he wasn't thinking of him as Talk-Talk anymore. Whenever he thought of him now it was Doc. It was all right to go, he would think; everyone has to go. But he didn't want him yanking his rug. That was really dying alone. Even if you died with no one around, with only the tubes, it still wasn't as alone.

He would go in to see him a few times a day. But the captain had avoided talking for so long, had kept distant for so long, that even though he wanted to talk now it was as though he couldn't. His tongue seemed to have grown so thick it filled his mouth, almost his whole head. Generally the most he would say was, "Hey," and stand there and wait for Doc to look at him. Then he would nod at him, as if he were just checking, that's all, and leave.

Because Doc wasn't looking up today he added, "What's up?" This time Doc did look up. He mumbled something.

"Can't hear you."

"Nothing's up," he said softly. "All down. Spirits, prick, everything."

"What's . . . wrong?"

He smiled for just an instant. He looked drunk. "Kidding? Talking to you forever, now what's wrong. Whyn't you join the staff? Only one person," he held up a finger, "understood. Got canned. Maybe skiddood. Captain, were you a dick?"

He nodded.

"Thought you was Navy. Been together how long, didn't hit me till now you might be a dick. Time to skiddoo, Captain. Kids don't want you, people don't listen, time to skiddoo. Older'n Mom and Pop. Remember my last words. I was twenty-two touched my first titty. A student nurse. So pretty. So pretty, pretty, pretty."

The captain stood there as Doc's head began to drop. He walked out, then looked back at the room. He once saw a man go from twenty-eight floors. He saw a kid put a revolver in his mouth and fire. He saw another kid hanging from a station house cell. He held the grocery store lady, Mrs. DiGregario, as she screamed, "I didn't believe him! I didn't believe him!" He was there when they lifted the garage doors and saw through the haze that stare from the front seat. He saw them in water, in the ground, in sand, in a closet, in a motel, a hotel, even in a boys' room near a school gym. He also stood on the girder of a bridge and talked a man back when his own priest couldn't. He pulled a gun from a woman's rising hand, ran carrying another woman to be pumped. Talked to people, all kinds, some who may have been bluffing and some not. And never lost one.

He didn't have any way to reach Doc now and couldn't trust himself to string together all the words. Yet all he wanted to say was: don't let them do this to you too.

He strode over to the station, to Reds.

"Gonna kill himself. Doc."

"Doc's going to kill himself?" She was clipping papers together and sticking them into folders. But eventually she did walk around and go to his door. "Doc, what's this about you killing yourself? You going to do that to us? You going to give this place a bad name? Doc, look at your robe. Come on, let me fix it."

She went into his room. After a little while she was back. She seemed unconcerned, continued putting the papers into folders.

"Get a doc!"

She looked up as though she had forgotten he was there. "Captain, will you just cool it? I'm going to call the doctor. All he's got is a little fever."

When the captain looked in again, Doc was in bed. Then soon after he returned from dinner he saw Dr. Benny go into the room. He looked on from the doorway. Benny was sitting on the bed, taking a stethoscope out of his bag. Reds was with him. Benny, looking over, said, "You go along, Captain. We'll take care of him."

"Wants to kill himself."

"Just run along, don't worry. Doc," he said, turning back, "what's all this talk I hear?"

The captain lingered outside his own room, watching. About five minutes later Benny came out, walked over to the station and wrote something on a pad, which he handed to Reds.

"How's it going, Captain?" he said, walking by.

At first the captain thought it was No Voice's snoring that woke him, then he realized the sounds were coming from the hall. He slid out of bed and peered out.

Several staff members and two uniformed police officers were clustered outside Doc's door. He started to walk toward them but one of the officers waved him back. Then he saw one of the nurses holding a knotted sheet that dangled to the floor. He went into his room, felt in back of him in the darkness for the mattress, lowered himself onto the edge. He sat there staring, feeling nothing for a while. Then it was as though the veins in his temples were responding to a drum.

You're now on death row, Benny.

27

The ringing of the phone woke David a little before seven in the morning.

"This is Lou Cummings." The administrator's voice had a tremor to it. "Look, we had a suicide during the night. Dr. Persky."

"Persky?"

"Yeah. It's terrible. They called me over, but I didn't see any point calling you in the middle of the night. But you're to call the medical examiner's office. They need some more stuff on him."

"Jesus. Jesus Christ."

"First a murder, now this. Do we have the luck?"

"David, what is it?" Laura was sitting up in bed.

"How did he do it?"

"It's really terrible," Cummings said. "He couldn't get out of bed without help, you know. What he did, he tied a sheet around one side of the bed frame and rolled off the other side. The fucken rails weren't up. From now on, everyone rails! The cops said they never saw anything like it. Had to be real desperate. Thank God, he left a note, it's to his kids and it's his handwriting all right. Still, there's gonna be an investigation. Thank God for the note though. I see in his chart he was depressed. He *was* depressed, right?"

"He was depressed."

"Thank God. That would be something, another murder."

"He threatened suicide."

"Thank God. Best news yet."

"Look, I'll come over."

"You can, but there's no point right now. He's at the morgue. You're to call the medical examiner, though."

"Who committed suicide?" Laura said when he hung up.

"Someone at the home. A doctor."

"A doctor killed himself?"

"A patient! He was a patient!"

"How did he do it?"

"What the hell's the difference?" he said, stripping off his pajamas, getting into his shorts.

"Why are you taking this out on me?"

"I'm sorry. It's . . . just a hell of a shock. He hung himself. What he did really was strangle himself. He couldn't stand up, so he knotted a sheet around his neck and around the bed frame and rolled off the other side. It's absolutely horrible. It had to be so slow. How he didn't scream, make noise. Maybe no one heard him."

"Dear God."

He washed his face. He was in no mood to shave—could get away with it anyway. She watched him as he got dressed.

"How old was he?"

"I think seventy-eight. I've gone sort of blank. He was alone, kids were far away. Had cancer of the colon, though they caught it in time, I think. And he'd had a stroke. He'd go off now and then, but most of the time he was clear."

"David," she said slowly, "can I ask you something? How do they know someone didn't kill him and make it look like a suicide?"

"They'll be checking that out. But he left a note. Laura," he said, looking straight at her, "he told me he was going to kill himself. He told me last evening. I saw him and he told me. He's been depressed for so long, he was always talking about how depressed he was—I didn't take it all that seriously. I had a little talk with him, but I didn't think he would really do it."

"David, you can't blame yourself. You can't stop people from killing themselves if they really want to. He was old and sick and alone and he saw it as his only way out. Look, about today. I don't have to leave today. I can go tomorrow."

"Don't be silly. I'm all right." She was going to be spending several days in New York with Karen. He might meet them there. "I'm going to head off to the plant."

"No breakfast?"

"I'll have something there. I'm really not hungry. Oh, I have to call the medical examiner. I'll call from there."

"David, try not to be upset. Promise me."

"Promise. Look, I'll call and let you know if I'm coming up. I probably will."

"Please. We'll have a good time."

"Give my love to Karen." He kissed her quickly on the lips. "Have a good time. I'll probably see you."

Usually his first move after starting the car was to turn on the stereo. But he was too troubled. He knew what you were supposed to do if a patient was depressed, spoke of suicide; he had read all the articles; had even applied them when he was in practice. Give them your time. Let them talk about their problems. Let them know you take them seriously. Ask if they have an actual plan. Weigh what you hear. And if you have any reason to think they might do it, see that they're watched or hospitalized or see a psychiatrist. *Something.* And though it was true you couldn't stop anyone who really wanted to die, very often you could. Just by listening, giving them support, letting them know they're important to you.

The thing was to try.

"Come on, Doc, don't talk like that. Everything will look brighter tomorrow."

That just about summed up what he had said to him. Cheer up, Doc. See you, Doc. We'll get that fever down, Doc.

He wanted desperately to speak to Pat. But he didn't even know where she was: he had called her twice this week, and between trying hoped she would call him. Yet he didn't know what he really wanted of her.

What would he say to her if he spoke to her now? Doc Persky killed himself; I didn't take him seriously; tell me it wasn't my fault.

The streets were filling up with cars heading into center city. He tried concentrating on his driving, then on the clinic. They were having a great deal of success with their classes on cardiopulmonary resuscitation. And the obesity program was going well. He wondered if he would get approval to offer flu shots again.

Thoughts of Doc crept in.

Christ, was he trying to drive himself crazy?

He couldn't have saved him. And even if he had saved him, saved him for what?

He had to put this in its right place. He was doing what he could for them. But that didn't mean giving up his sanity, his physical health, his life.

Checking Yorky's record, LaSala remembered him quite well. And it put a downer on his hopes. Whatever he had done, Yorky had never resorted to violence.

Whoever was behind this was a crazy; not only didn't Yorky's history fit that but, when LaSala and Goldner visited him in his apartment, they instinctively felt: *nope.* He was an ordinary working stiff with a pleasant-looking young wife; he spoke quite calmly, rationally.

"Look, I don't know what this is all about. I like the captain—I love the guy—and we had him over here once, and once we took him out for a ride. Now, I don't know about any murders. I see a murder in the paper I don't even read about it. I met all those bums I ever want to meet. I don't want to read about them."

Goldner said, "Let's talk about some dates. Now, the first one was the night of July sixth. You happen to remember that night?"

"You're talking over two months ago. How would I remember two months ago?"

"The night of July twenty-ninth."

"Come on now. Geez."

"All right, three weeks ago, August twenty-fifth."

"What kind a day was that?"

"A Friday. Friday night."

"Friday." He thought, then looked at his wife. He smiled. "Vickie, you tell 'em. I want it from you, not from me."

She thought. "We were at the Noonans', right?"

"Tell 'em."

"We were at these friends of ours, the Noonans'. They had us up for the weekend."

"When to when?"

"It's a hundred-mile drive—no, more than that—we got there Friday afternoon and we come back Sunday."

"You didn't work Friday?" LaSala asked Yorky.

"You can check. No. And I'll give you the Noonans' phone number, address. Ask 'em. In fact, they had people over for dinner."

Closing the door, Yorky stood holding the knob, thinking.

Victoria said, "Yorky, you ain't in trouble, are you?"

"Oh Christ, no."

But he was thinking about the captain, about his taking the car. He didn't know what night that was, but he had the car.

The captain a killer? Oh Jesus, no. But he'd had the car, whatever night that was.

The cops had never asked him, so he hadn't said anything. And he wouldn't. Ever.

Then he remembered something. He'd had to give the nurse at the front desk his name each time he had taken him out. She had written it into a book. And that must have the date.

What if they checked that and came back?

He would still never mention the car. But what about Vickie? How could he ask her to lie? How could he involve her?

When they got back to headquarters, Goldner called the state police to have them check on the Noonans. The report came back in an hour.

The Noonans and two other couples had confirmed the Yorkys' story.

LaSala had expected this, but had been hoping. Now where?

28

He couldn't find any Dr. Benny in the telephone book. He had the feeling it wasn't his right name, that it just sounded something like that, but he looked anyway. He kept twisting his glasses, turning his head, as though somehow that would make the name pop up from the book.

He hated going back to his room because he hated going past Doc's. He missed him, the yapping, the growl, the cigar, even the goddamn cap.

He wished Benny would just come in. He would get his gun, and no matter where he met up with him, in the hall, the dining room, anywhere, just so long as no one else got hurt, no matter where it was he would pull the switch. He didn't care about hiding or getting away. He just wanted him dead so he couldn't hurt anyone else.

Should he ask Reds what his real name was? He walked up to her at the station. It was several moments before she noticed him.

"You want something, Captain?"

He was thinking: If I ask they'll get suspicious, I'll lose him.

"Do you want something?"

He shook his head, his gaze going past her now. On the wall in back of her was a sheet of paper. It had a heading typed on it: STAFF

PHYSICIANS. Under that were names, though he couldn't make out the names from here.

He shuffled away from the station.

"Ruthie! Ruthie!" Sporty still rocking by his window, forever calling out her name now.

He went back to his room, stood in the doorway looking at the station. Wasn't she ever going to leave? He wondered should he go into his room and wait there; she might wonder why he was looking. But she was starting to stand up now. He walked closer. She spotted him approaching.

"You want something, Captain?"

He shook his head. She went to the medicine cart. She came back to the station and stood there looking down at something on the counter. After several moments she straightened up, smiled at him, and went into one of the rooms.

He edged around the counter. Then he shot one hand out, grabbed the sheet, stuffed it in his pocket. He had torn part of it; a small piece remained scotch-taped to the wall. He wanted to leap for it, it seemed to stand out like a face, but he saw Reds coming back. He started walking away.

Near his room he turned to see if she had noticed it, but she was sitting down, facing the hall. In his room he saw that he had only ripped off the heading and part of one of the names.

There were only four names on it, under each a telephone number.

Ah. Bennett. David J. Bennett, M fucken D. And two numbers. One said "Clinic," one said "Home."

He went up the hall to the phone booths. He wanted addresses, not phone numbers. But there were two million Bennetts and a half a million David Bennetts in the book. And three David Bennetts, M.D., but, ah, only one David J. He worked his pencil carefully on the paper he placed flat on the open book. Two-o-three-seven Everwood.

Back in his room, looking out at the night, he wondered when he should go. He would go right now. Except.

Where was Everwood?

He knew that street, he knew it, he knew it. But he didn't know it. He couldn't think where it came in. He used to know where it came in, he knew every goddamn street in this whole goddamn city, but he couldn't think, he couldn't think.

He was so frustrated, so angry, he couldn't fall asleep. Finally he was able to after consoling himself that someday that bastard had to come in. He would get his gun and, so help him God, wherever.

He woke sometime in the dead of night. He felt as if he'd had a good dream because he felt relaxed—and without his consciously striving for it, it came to him. He knew exactly where Everwood came in.

But he wouldn't tomorrow. He knew that like he knew where Everwood was right now. He crept out of bed and fished around for a pencil in his pants hanging in the closet. Then he found the paper on which he had jotted down the address. He drew a couple of lines. One line he marked MASON S. Then, near where the two lines intersected, he marked EVERWOOD S. And again near the intersection, because he remembered even this, he printed 3D CENTRL BNK.

The next evening he was ready to go right after dinner. But people were always out in the parking lot whenever he looked. He would have to wait again until late, slip out the side. But tonight it took longer than ever. It was after ten before he was able to make it across the hall. And when he got outside he had a jolt. One of the parked cars had its lights on.

Whoever was in there was probably waiting for someone to come out. So come out, will you?

Ten minutes must have passed, maybe more. He didn't want to go back in, wait another night. He thought: maybe I'll go anyway; maybe it's someone who won't recognize me, will think it's my car. But that was too risky, could mean losing the bastard!

Wait, boys, just wait. I'll tell you when.

He touched the gun in his belt to reassure himself it was still there. He had loaded it again: it had six in the chamber, and there were five more, all that was left, in the box in his pants pocket. He wasn't wearing his jacket tonight. Too hot, too much to do. No encumbrances, Gordie that great jig sergeant of his used to say.

Soon, frowning, he became aware of something about that car.

Maybe he was getting deaf, but he couldn't hear a motor. He sidled along the building, to get as close to it as he could. No, that motor just wasn't on. He could even hear crickets. Either a couple was in there doing what they shouldn't and didn't think about the lights, or someone had left it parked with the lights on.

No one doing what they shouldn't in there would forget about lights, would they?

He inched away from the shadows of the building. Boys, let's go.

He broke across the lot, to the rock, pulled it aside. Gripping the keys, he moved from hood to hood. Now, in the car, he started it easily. Out of the driveway, the lights on, he headed toward the street, he didn't remember its name but was sure he would know it, that would take him to Mason Street.

He found that street and afterward Mason, though suddenly he didn't know whether to go right or left on it. He decided on left. As he was driving he saw a police car parked at a curb, two officers in it. He told himself to just keep going, but something broke in him and he turned into a side street, and then another. And regretted it instantly. Even the dumbest rookie in the world would pick that up. He quickly pulled into an open spot in a line of cars parked along the curb, turned off the motor and lights, then went low in the seat.

He thought of word being radioed back to the Pistol, that ruthless bastard ordering out more cars. He remained low, waiting. Occasionally a car would go by and he would raise up a little, but none had their lights flashing. He started the motor, waited just a while longer, then pulled out. Now he had to find Mason Street again. He made a series of turns, frantic that none seemed right. Then, like an old friend waiting, there it was. Again the decision to go right or left; again left, but it felt wrong and yet he was afraid to get caught making a u-turn. He kept going. And just ahead of him he saw the bank.

You could only go one way on Everwood, and as he drove he kept trying to make out the addresses. The houses were turning from twins into singles and then into larger singles, the numbers in the sixteens now, then the seventeens. He stopped once and got out to look at a number on a lantern, and it was in the twenty-threes and he knew he had passed it by a few blocks. He drove back on a parallel street, cut to Everwood again, and found the twenty block. He got out and walked up driveways to see if he could find the numbers. Three driveways and he had 2037.

The house was dark, there were no cars in the driveway. The garage had windows and he peered in. No cars there, either. Hand on his gun, he rang the doorbell. No answer.

Wrong house? Were they on vacation?

He walked down the driveway toward the street and this time he saw a mailbox on a post. It had a little sign under it. It was so dark he could only make out a few letters on it, but a couple of them were enough: M.D. Also he saw some mail in the box.

Unless they were a-holes it meant they weren't on vacation. Only a-holes didn't stop the mail.

He wondered what to do. If he drove his car in here it would, of course, warn them when they returned. It wasn't so smart even keeping it parked where it was.

He went back to the car and drove into a little street, parked it and walked back. He started testing windows. Every goddamn one he could reach was locked. He went to the back door. Locked too. By now his eyes were fully accustomed to the dark, and he could make out some kind of slanty door that apparently led down to the basement. He found the handle and turned it and was able to lift it. He lowered it slowly behind him. Then he felt around the underside of the door and found what he hoped, a sliding bolt. It was stiff, probably rusty, but he worked it loose and shoved it in place. He tested the door, tried to push it open—but it was locked now.

Hoping this was the only entrance to the basement, he found he was wrong. He had to go down a few steps. Here was the final door to it. But they were a-holes, after all. He could feel framed glass, even near the knob. He took out his gun and tapped one of the windows with the butt. He did it too lightly; it must have cracked but it didn't break. None of the neighbors could hear, it was almost forever between houses, but he was still afraid to hit it too hard. He took a deep breath and smashed it, then smashed at the shards remaining in the frame. Then he stiffened. Somewhere in the distance, as though across a field, a dog began barking. He waited until it stopped. Then he reached in, found the lock, turned it.

In the basement he walked gingerly in the dark. There was a little moonlight coming through a few small windows, but not enough to keep him from floundering, from bumping into things. He walked with one arm extended. Finally, he touched some carpeted steps. He made his way up them. The door at the top, to the kitchen, was unlocked.

He was sitting, now, in what he guessed was the living room. He took the gun from his belt and put it on his lap. Doing that just seemed to take his last strength. He leaned back, listening to his heart, his breathing.

Not bad for an old guy, eh Gordie?

29

The car was reported stolen soon after the three-to-eleven shift went off duty. They didn't know the captain was missing until he didn't show up for breakfast and they checked his room. They didn't connect him with the missing car, thought he had wandered off again. After all, he was a wanderer. And so they followed their usual, quick routine: while some of the staff drove through the neighborhood, others looked through the basement and into closets.

When they didn't find him within fifteen minutes Cummings made the two calls he hated to make because it reflected on the home. He called the local police station and gave them his description. And he called the son.

"How could he disappear like that?" Mark demanded.

"I know you're upset, but we'll find him. He can't be very far."

"How could he have gotten out?"

"He wasn't in restraints, Mr. Hughes, and he can walk."

"Well, why the hell wasn't he in restraints? Isn't someone near the door? How could he get past them?"

"Once in a blue moon they do get past."

"I'm coming down!"

Hanging up, Cummings turned wearily to the director of nurses. "He wants to know why he wasn't in restraints. Can we ever satisfy families? When they're in restraints they get upset. And if they're not, and fall or wander off, they're on your neck. Where the hell *is* he?"

"Mr. Cummings," she said, "I've been thinking something which I've hesitated to say. I was hoping he'd show up by now. What if whoever murdered Kay kidnapped him?"

"For Christ's sake, what're you trying to do to me? Why they want to kidnap *him*?"

"I don't know. I'm just saying."

"That's absolutely crazy!" He kept looking at her, then picked up the phone again. This time he asked for the number of police headquarters.

The call was transferred to Inspector McDowell, who immediately called in Denny and LaSala. The inspector said, "Look, there are a lot of possibilities here. One, and this is the most likely, it has nothing at all to do with the murders. Two, it's someone at the home who thinks the old man knows too much and might be able to spout it out some day. If that's it he's dead. Now, the third. Look, I know this is nuts, but is he able to drive?"

"Inspector," Denny said, "five people have been murdered in three sections of the city. The nurse was near the home. That could be. But the others? This is an old man in a nursing home."

"Can he still drive?"

LaSala picked up the phone. "Get me a Mark Hughes. No, I don't know the address. Wait, never mind."

He hurried into his office and got the son's phone number. Soon he was speaking to Mark's wife. "Lieutenant, my husband's at the nursing home. They called us. He's missing."

"Yes, I know. Tell me. Do you know if the old man was driving a car before he went into the home?"

"He hasn't driven for years. His children made him stop."

He hung up. "She says he hasn't driven for years. Look, let's get there."

They found his son and daughters standing near the front desk. They looked desperate. Mark said, "Most Pop's clothes are still in his room. I'm sure that means he didn't mean to leave. He's got to be wandering around somewhere."

LaSala, followed by Goldner, went to his room. He searched through the coat and jacket pockets, came out with some papers. He worked at straightening them. The first one he read was the will. He handed it to Goldner. As he read on he began to frown; then he went cold.

> *Officil Report. She cried when L. said gone send you state and I pleeded with bitch. Dont ever kick out old. I believe in capitol punishmnt. A deterint. No one ought die alone. Old poor no place to live. Two gilty as one. Cop got to ride. Never say yr crazi. They said to him yr crazi. Hs mony. Capitol punishment deterint.*

There were a few more lines, but he could only make out the same word: *deterint.*

Goldner, seeing him standing there stunned, took the paper from him.

"No one, no one," LaSala said, "is going to make me believe someone else isn't in it. Sid, get Yorky. I want to talk to him again." He went out to the hall, said to a nurse, "I want to see Captain Hughes' chart."

"I'll have to get permission."

"Please get it for me, will you?"

She brought it to him and he began reading.

"Do you have any idea where my father is?" Mark was saying.

"No." He kept reading.

"Rosie," Mark said, "now stop crying. He's going to be all right."

LaSala went into a room by himself to finish it. When he came out he strode over to the inspector. His hand was quivering as he showed him a page on the chart. "This is unreal. None of this is happening. Remember the investment broker who got off? The captain was in restraints the week the story broke."

"Look, where the Christ is he?"

"I'll add his description to the alarm on the car." He motioned to Cummings. "Who owns that car?"

"The stolen car? Miss Tomley. She doesn't come on till three."

"Someone get her on the phone for me."

Several minutes later he was talking to her. "Did Captain Hughes ever ask to borrow your car?"

"Who?"

"Captain Hughes."

"Of course not. He's a patient."

"I know that. And I know you wouldn't loan it to him. But did he ever ask?"

"No."

"What happened last night? Did you leave your keys in it?"

"No, I've got them. I'm looking right at them. I—" She paused. "You know, I just remembered something. I lost my keys about a month, a month and a half ago."

LaSala could feel the perspiration running from him as he stood at the nursing station, his hand still on the cradled phone. Then he saw Goldner coming in.

"Got Yorky at work. He's at headquarters. He said the night he took the captain home the captain asked to borrow his car. Believe this or not, he said he never asked him any questions. Just gave him the keys. He said he doesn't know the date, but he had to log out."

Going through the names and dates in the book, they soon learned when this was.

LaSala, grimacing, asked for a couple aspirins; even his eyes seemed to be pulsating. Now that he had gotten through most of the shock, and the anger at being made a fool of, he couldn't help it he felt sorry for that poor old demented son of a bitch. But that was easy to put away.

He was too worried about whomever, God help them, the captain was after now.

He woke up, startled, blinking at the sunlight. It hurt just to raise his head. Probably from climbing up that ladder, then crawling up the slanty roof to the skylight. And it had been a long drop from the skylight to the floor.

You O.K., Joe?

I'm O.K., Captain.

Gordie?

Just fine, Captain.

They were good boys, all of them.

He began to see with some surprise that he was lying on his back somewhere, not on his side; that he was on a sofa, not a floor. And the bare room in a factory was changing to a living room.

They ought to be here soon, Gordie said.

How long we been here?

I'd say twenty-two hours, Gordie said.

He sat up. He saw that he was alone. He wondered, deeply worried, if he had actually spoken. He didn't want his memory to go. Not now, not now. Did you actually know when it started to go completely?

He went into the kitchen, fully aware where he was, who he wanted; still he was somewhat worried. He opened the refrigerator, saw a bottle of orange juice and filled up a glass. He downed it with a few long swallows. Felt better, much better.

He looked around the first floor for a bathroom and found it. He'd been in a lot worse places than this. Once went a whole day without being able to take a piss. He went to the front window of the living room and peered out a slight fold at one end of the closed drapes. The driveway was empty, the sun bright. He sat down on a heavily cushioned chair, holding the gun on his lap.

He knew the name perfectly now. Bennett. This eased his concern about his memory. Bennett.

Daddy, guess where I am, Rosemarie called from behind the dune.

He knew he was just thinking that. He smiled slightly at the memory, remembered how he had made believe he couldn't find her.

Captain, with this commendation I speak for the people of this city in offering their thanks, the mayor said. He knew he was just thinking of that, too. He had one hundred and sixty-eight official commendations. Sometimes they came from the mayor, most times from the commissioner—he had seen commissioners come and go—and sometimes just through the mail.

Will you take as your bride?

They went to Rehoboth Beach, Delaware, for their honeymoon, in an old Ford. They were the only honeymoon couple he ever met, the clerk said, who took along a dog. Ruff, you better close your eyes. Did he say that or Josie?

Daddy, why do you have hair on your chest and not on your head? Rosemarie. Actually, all of them at one time or another.

Still, just thinking. It helped time go, kept him loose. He checked the gun to make sure again it was fully loaded.

He thought of Tommy Jenkins who could do more to a door with his foot than you could with a hammer. He thought of Vince Gombaro that time, unshaven but wearing a dress in that park with the rapes. He thought of Gordie, spread out on the sidewalk, that big square face expressionless in death as in life, a little red hole by the side of his nose. A nothing job, yet Gordie dead. Was it eighteen years?

He forced his thoughts away from that. He wanted to be completely here now, fully alert, ready. Bennett.

What's that about a warrant?

I said I don't have it, Captain, you got it? Gordie said.

Ah, Gordie. Would I be here without a warrant?

The three-to-eleven shift was coming on. LaSala saw a red-haired nurse take over the station. "What's wrong? What's the matter?" she asked.

"Captain Hughes is missing."

"Missing?"

"Since last night. I'd like to ask you a few questions."

"Sure."

"Do you know of any quarrels he's had with anyone lately?"

"Well, he can be ornery. But I've never seen him quarrel with a patient, if that's what you mean. He gives us some hell, but I've never seen him raise hell with a patient. And you do see some of that go on once in a while. Someone doesn't want someone else to sit next to him. Someone accuses someone of stealing. Mostly they sit by themselves, they ignore each other, but you see things go on. I know that he was upset a couple nights ago. A patient over there, that room, committed suicide. Doc Persky. The odd thing is, the captain knew he would. Doc Persky told him he would, and the captain told us—but I wasn't on when he killed himself. They found him about two in the morning."

"You say he told us? Who's *us*?"

"Well, I know at least me and the doctor. I was in the room with the doctor when he was examining Doc Persky. And the captain stood over there and he said something like, 'He wants to kill himself.'"

"Which doctor is that?"

"Dr. Bennett. He's the captain's doctor also."

"Where can I get hold of him?"

"Well, his number is—" She turned, then stopped. She pointed, startled, at the torn piece of paper on the wall.

Goldner quickly strode to the office to get the phone numbers.

LaSala called after him, "Call all the doctors."

Goldner was back in a few minutes. "I was able to reach all but one. Bennett. Dr. Kliegman said Bennett asked him to take over for him yesterday. He said he was going to New York to join his wife and daughter. He's supposed to be back today."

30

Every so often he would go over and peer through the drapes. It not only gave him a good view of the driveway but also the front steps. He also would go into the kitchen now and then and look out from there. He couldn't see how anyone could sneak in the back without him knowing; they would have to come up the drive. Still, you couldn't take that chance.

Most of the time he sat in the living room, near the baby grand. The way he figured it, as soon as he heard the car pull up he would either duck behind the baby grand and wait until he came into the living room, or duck behind that big chair over there that faced the front door.

But what if he didn't show? What if he'd taken a long vacation?

The longest they'd ever had to wait, if he remembered right, was fifty-two hours. And Irv stayed right with them, even though it ran into one of his holidays when he couldn't eat anything.

Irv, Vince said, how come you didn't become a doctor?

My mother wouldn't let me. She always dreamed of me being a cop.

Even Gordie had smiled. You never saw Gordie smile too often.

Which reminded him about food. His stomach was beginning to rumble. It was easy to forget about eating when you were on a job. But that could put you at a big disadvantage. The guy coming in could be well rested and well fed, and here you were suddenly with the food shakes.

Anyone bring anything along?

I got chewing gum, Vince said.

I got this little blueberry pie, Gordie said. Here, I'll break it.

He did want a piece of that pie, just something to swallow. But as he began to reach for it, he made himself shake Gordie and Vince and all the rest of them away. They weren't here, and he couldn't let them in again. They were good boys, oh, great boys all of them, but they weren't here, they were only getting in the way.

He was just about finished when the phone rang. It seemed to be ringing throughout the house. It was a startling sound, it was as if someone were in the house, and he came out to the living room again and stood watching the phone there, one of its buttons glittering like an eye. After seven or so rings it stopped. Somehow, it made the house quieter than ever; a thick kind of quiet that took him back to his house as a kid when he would come in on a summer day, sweaty from a game and no one home.

He was growing more edgy, but it was nowhere near fear. The only worry he had about himself was that something might happen to keep him from doing his job. He remembered that time he heard the guys he was after had a contract on him. That was his only worry then, too. For maybe three weeks, until he grabbed them, he used to start his car by putting his arm through the window and turning the ignition. That was nuts, it would have blown all of him anyway; still, you did the best you could.

Josie, though she never said anything, used to watch from their door.

He thought: maybe it would be best from the baby grand. Bennett would close the door and come to this archway opening from the hall to the living room. No, the chair. That would be best. He could get him just coming in the door.

He was frowning, thinking he heard a car. Then he was sure of it. But he could tell it was more than one car. He was crouched in the center of the room. He could hear car doors opening and closing. Gun extended, he crawled over to the chair. From there he could see the knob turning. Then someone began pushing at the door, trying to force it—just for a few seconds. He could hear voices at both sides of the house, a rattling at each window, then the voices going toward the back, then to the front again. Silence, then voices again, this time farther away as though whoever they were wanted to get a full view of the house.

He was sure they were the Pistol's men.

He had done that ten million times, testing doors, windows, wondering. He could even picture some of them leaning back against their cars, arms crossed, maybe legs, looking, thinking.

He took the box of cartridges out of his pocket and put it on the floor next to him. He was suddenly aware that his hands were trembling and cold. It came as a little shock, as if he'd become unfit for a job. It was good to be nervous, anxious, but just enough not to take crazy chances; you can't shake, for Christ's sake.

He sat there, eyes closed, listening to the sound of his breathing, trying to steady himself.

Just this one job. Let him hang onto it long enough for just this job.

. . . Were they going?

He was breathing so hard he wasn't sure what he heard. But now he knew it was a motor. He inched his way over to the corner of the drape, saw a car backing out. He also saw part of another car. And this one didn't move.

Probably one of the cars had gotten a call to another job.

He remembered how it used to be. Four or five cars would be heading to a job or parked all around a place, and you'd think this was the only job in the world, then a call would come through and one or two would have to peel off.

God, there wasn't a thing those guys out there ever thought or felt or did that he never thought or felt or did! God, he was a cop! Didn't they know he was . . . just a cop?

He let the drape fall back into place and sat near it, his back against the side wall, his legs straight out, hand over the gun.

His thoughts began to drift. He found himself wondering whatever happened to Mary.

A short while later he was jolted alert, was sitting up straight again. Another car was pulling in. He peered through the drapes, had to wait until it came into view. It wasn't, he saw, one of the Pistol's cars, it was a fancy job. He couldn't see where it was parked, but again he could hear doors open and close. Now he could make out voices over there, somewhere to his right. He strained to see, couldn't.

There was silence now.

Then he saw two figures walking toward the front steps.

He scrambled over to the chair to kneel behind it, but suddenly everything went dark in his head and he seemed to be spinning within it, and his legs were starting to crumble. He grabbed hold of the chair, remembering in panic this happening once at the home and someone telling him not to get up so fast next time, the blood leaves your head. He was going under, he felt himself going, and he sagged to his knees; but as his head fell forward to his chest the darkness began to lift a little, the spinning was slowing, he was becoming aware of his body again, that he had a heart that was beating, had shoulders, a chest, arms, that he was intact, kneeling in place behind the chair, that he was feeling stronger, much stronger now, that he was holding a gun.

He kept his head down, in control of himself now, waiting.

His shirt was icy wet with sweat.

There. And he raised his head a little, peered around the side of the chair. The sound of a key in the lock. It was working the lock forever, but now the door opened and he saw trousers, and he let them come closer, just a little closer, and he stood up, both hands on the gun, and there were two men, one of them *him.* He fired once at him, then swung the gun at the other, a face he seemed to remember, and he motioned him into the living room with the gun and the other came, someone he knew, someone from where, one of the boys.

Hey, it was one of the boys.

He lowered the gun slowly.

He heard, for the briefest moment in time, the roar.

31

LaSala's hands were trembling so much he couldn't get his gun into the holster. He shoved it under his belt.

Someone, leaning over the captain, said, "He's gone."

The captain was lying on his back, his legs bent to one side, eyes wide, blood gushing from a hole in his right temple. LaSala stared at him dazedly, then back at the doctor. The doctor had fallen into a sitting position. His arms were folded hard over his stomach, blood seeping through, his eyes flickering at his wife who was screaming. He shook his head fiercely as someone tried to prop him up.

A police emergency wagon was there within minutes, soon was speeding off with the doctor and his wife. Other police cars had raced in; still others, from the sound of sirens, were coming.

Goldner was doing the talking for LaSala, was telling the inspector that the other men had left while he and the lieutenant waited for the doctor and his wife. Jesus, they had no idea the captain was in there.

Another police wagon drew up. There was none of the hurry of the first. The two officers who got out spoke to the inspector, then opened the rear doors and drew out a stretcher. LaSala watched them walk into the house. There was a ball of nausea low in his stomach. They were bringing out the stretcher, the shoes protruding from the sheet. LaSala turned away quickly. There was a bitter little cluster at the back of his throat, but he managed to swallow it down. Why was he shivering?

"Go home," the inspector said.

"No."

"I said go home."

"Come on," Goldner said, "I'll drop you off."

Goldner opened the door, stood there looking at him until he climbed in. Then Goldner closed the door and came around and started the car. They drove, saying nothing.

After about a mile, LaSala said, staring straight ahead, "I didn't have to shoot him."

"I don't hear a word you say."

"I didn't have to shoot him."

"You tell anyone, you're a schmuck. You did him a favor."

They drove silently. The sun glittered on the hood.

"Do it for me some day," Goldner said.